R

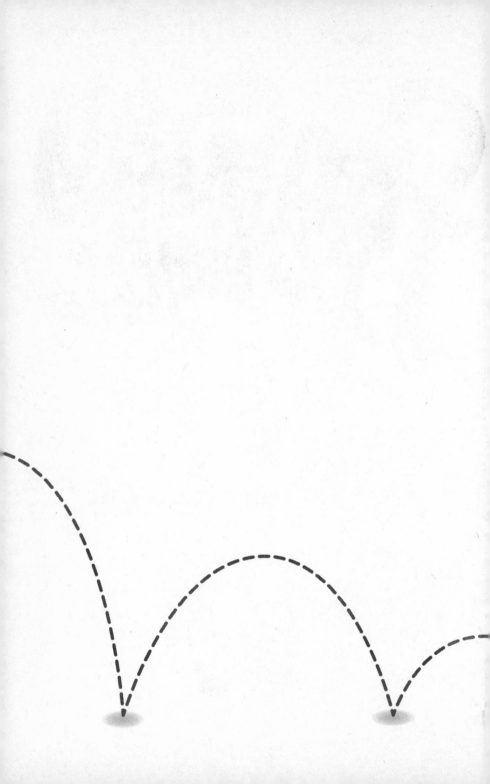

fenway and Hattie*

Victoria J. Coe

G. P. PUTNAM'S SONS

G. P. PUTNAM'S SONS
an imprint of Penguin Random House LLC
375 Hudson Street, New York, NY 10014

Library of Congress Cataloging-in-Publication Data
Coe, Victoria J.
Fenway and Hattie / Victoria J. Coe.
pages cm
Summary: "An excitable Jack Russell terrier named Fenway and his Favorite
Short Human, Hattie, move to the suburbs and must adjust to the changes that
come with their new home"—Provided by publisher.
[1. Jack Russell terrier—Fiction. 2. Dogs—Fiction. 3. Human-animal
relationships—Fiction. 4. Moving, Household—Fiction.] I. Title.
PZ7.1.C635Fe 2016
[Fic]—dc23
2015009117

Printed in the United States of America.
ISBN 978-0-399-17274-8
1 3 5 7 9 10 8 6 4 2

Design by Ryan Thomann.
Text set in Chaparral.

To Philip, James, and Ralph,
for sharing the joys, humor,
and challenges of loving a dog,

and to Kipper,
for the endless inspiration

CHAPTER 1

As soon as we get off the elevator, I know something is wrong. Our apartment has no mat in front. The muddy boots and fake flowers are gone. The doorway looks empty. Abandoned. Like nobody lives here.

Who took our stuff? Intruders? Strangers?

Squirrels?!

Fetch Man opens the door, and I race inside. Nose to the floor, I sniff for clues. But all I smell are Food Lady, Fetch Man, and Hattie—my own family.

I rush into the Eating Place. Apparently, Food Lady is not aware that things are missing. She gives me a quick pat, then sighs, like she has a big job to do. She's completely focused on a pile of boxes.

Packages!

My tail goes nuts. I stick my snout in the closest box and begin rooting around. But it smells boring like old teacups, not new and exciting like a package.

"FEN-way," Food Lady scolds. That's Human for "You're in trouble!"

My ears droop, and I back away. I was only doing my job. Packages must be inspected. What if they're hiding something dangerous? Or delicious?

Fetch Man smiles and kisses Food Lady's cheek. He speaks quickly and gestures a lot. Like he's the happiest human in the world. What's he so excited about? Isn't he worried that our stuff's been stolen? Good thing my humans have a Jack Russell Terrier on patrol. We're obviously in terrible danger. There's so much to do!

I keep sniffing around, but I do not find one single clue. And no tasty crumbs or yummy drips, either. Food Lady wraps noisy paper around the dishes and tucks them into a big box. She grabs crinkly bags of chips and pretzels and cookies. Cans and jars, too. Pretty soon, the cabinets are cleared out. Hey, wait a minute! What are we supposed to eat?

I must warn my short human. I race to her room, barking the whole way. "Bad news, Hattie! We're going to starve!"

But when I get there, she's surrounded by boxes, too. And she looks miserable. Probably because she couldn't come to the Dog Park. Hattie loves playing ball and chase as much as I do.

Even though I have terrible news, she forgets how sad she is when she sees me. "Fenn-waay," she sings in her sweet voice. That means "Here's a treat."

"Hooray! Hooray!" I bark, blasting through the door. That's My Hattie, always thinking of me. I scamper over a box and hurl myself at her legs. "I can hardly wait!"

"Awww," she says with a giggle, reaching into her pocket. The treat sails into my mouth.

Chomp! Wowee, that hits the spot.

Hattie pats my head and gazes into my eyes, her face back to being sad. Like that was the very last treat.

"That's what I was saying, Hattie. We've been wiped out," I bark. "Probably by squirrels!"

Her shoulders sink with the horrible realization.

I nuzzle her ankle. "Don't worry. Your protector is here."

She must be feeling worse than I thought, because her dark eyes go right to the way-up-high shelf. She climbs onto the bed and reaches for the fuzzy toy that used to be a bear but is now only the upper half. With one arm.

Uh-oh! That means something scary is happening. Like a stormy night with rain and boom-kabooms.

Hattie pulls the used-to-be bear off the high shelf. She clutches it to her chest. She is scared.

Good thing I'm here to cheer her up! As she's stepping down, I snatch the used-to-be bear from her arms. I zip around the bed and fly over a box.

Hattie's on my tail, laughing. "Hey!" she says, reaching out her arms.

I'm just beyond her grasp. I'm hopping through a pile of shoes when I stumble over something hard. *Ouch!* My bedtime hairbrush. What's it doing on the floor?

Sensing opportunity, Hattie lunges. "Drop it!" she shouts in a voice that sounds anything but angry.

She's fast, but I'm faster. I spring onto the bed. I bury my nose in the rumpled blankets. They smell like mint and vanilla, just like she does.

Hattie flops down beside me, smiling. She takes the used-to-be bear and grabs me tight. "Best buddies," she coos. She kisses my brown paw, then my white paw. She showers my neck with kisses. Our favorite snuggle game!

I slobber her cheek as she giggles. She's the best short human ever.

Food Lady appears in the doorway. One hand's on her hip. The other's pointing at the boxes. "Hattie," she scolds.

Hattie's smile disappears. As she bolts up, I hop off her chest. She smells worried. I know how she feels.

I wait for Food Lady to start yelling in a bossy voice.

But instead, the words I hear are Hattie's. She sounds anxious. She picks up the long jump rope that she brings to the place where short humans with backpacks go. She shows Food Lady a card. I catch a whiff of hardened frosting from the time a pack of short humans invaded and I warned Hattie that her treats were on fire.

As Hattie goes on, Food Lady's angry face gets softer and softer. Until it's turned to sad. "Oh, bay-bee," she says in a soothing tone. She sits next to us on the bed.

Hattie leans into her arm. Food Lady strokes Hattie's bushy hair.

I nuzzle in under Food Lady's hand. "I could use a few strokes, too, you know," I whimper. "Right behind this ear."

Food Lady rocks us gently the way she did when Hattie's knee was hurt. She gives us both a pat and gets up. "Okay?" she asks.

Hattie nods and sniffles a few times. "Okay," she says. But I know she's still worried. Hattie's sad and scared and packing things. It reminds me of something. But what? If only I could think of it.

When Food Lady's gone, Hattie tosses the jump rope into a box. Then clothes—*whoosh*. And shoes—*clunk*. She picks up the used-to-be bear and squeezes it tight.

And then I remember what this reminds me of! It was right before Hattie disappeared for two whole nights.

And something terrible must've happened to her. Because when she finally came back, her clothes smelled horrible. Like burnt marshmallows and squirrels.

Oh no! Could it be happening again? I knew something was wrong!

Hattie is leaving! Hattie is leaving!

I spring up and run in circles. She can't go, at least not without her loyal dog. Hey! If I stick by her side, she'll have to take me with her. Wowee, it's the Best Idea Ever!

As Hattie turns from box to box, I'm on her like fur. When she closes the last one, she heads for the door. I beat her to it.

She leaps over me, and I chase her to the Eating Place. Food Lady's standing at the counter, licking her fingers. She looks up and holds out a white bag that smells like doughnuts. "Breck-fest," she calls.

"Yippee!" I bark, racing to Food Lady's feet. Hattie squeals, then grabs the bag and crinkles it open.

I leap on her legs and lick my chops.

Hattie bites into a squishy doughnut. A lovely glob of goo drips right into my mouth. *Mmmmm.* Vanilla. I swallow quickly. "More, please," I bark, jumping on her legs again.

Hattie giggles. But when Food Lady crosses her arms, she stops.

Right then, a rattling sounds at the front door. Intruders? I charge into the Lounging Place as the door swings open. I'm ready to pounce.

It's Fetch Man! He was gone? I spring up and paw his knees. "I missed you so much," I bark. "Is it playtime?"

But he's all business. And he's not alone.

A group of Large Strangers follows him in. One after another, they come through the door, reeking of coffee and sweat. A suspicious combination! And Fetch Man is not making one move to stop them.

"Hey! Who are you? Why are you here?" I bark, lunging toward them but stopping a safe distance from the first stranger. He is a lot bigger than Fetch Man.

"Shhhh," Fetch Man says. He grabs me by the collar and pulls me to the far side of the room.

"Watch out!" I bark. "These guys are probably dangerous!"

As if to prove my point, the Very Large Strangers begin lifting the boxes. One of them takes the Flashing Screen right off the wall.

"Can't you see they're stealing our stuff?" I bark, wiggling and kicking. "Let me go! I must be free to do my job!"

But my warnings aren't doing one bit of good. Fetch Man and Food Lady just stand there, watching these Evil Humans loot everything.

"Let me at 'em! Seriously, I can take these guys!" I pull. I twist. I'm desperate to get loose. I'm about to choke myself when Fetch Man deposits me into the Eating Place. "Can't you see what's happening?" I bark. "If you ever needed a dog to protect you, it's now!"

Unfazed, Fetch Man snaps The Gate across the doorway. I'm trapped! "What are you doing?" I bark. "Are you nuts?" I jump my highest, but I'm no match for The Gate.

I can't keep this up for long. My legs are getting tired and my bark is wearing out. Danger is happening right here in our home and all I can do is watch.

And worst of all, I got separated from Hattie when I was supposed to be sticking by her side. There goes the plan!

Chapter 2

It's going to be a lot of hard work, but I will not rest until I'm reunited with Hattie. I spin around and around. I stretch and leap up again and again. I race back and forth from one end of the Eating Place to the other, stopping only once to lick a tasty drip on the floor.

Mmmmm. Vanilla!

At last, there's only one thing left to do. I whine in my most pitiful voice. "Hey, everybody! Remember me? I'm all alone and I'm trapped."

Finally, my efforts pay off. Hattie rushes over, her

backpack strapped to her back. Her face is weary and happy at the same time. "Ready?" she asks.

"I'm so ready! I'm so ready!" I bark, my tail going wild. Hattie removes The Gate, and I sprint into the Lounging Place.

I'm too late! The Evil Humans are gone. And so is the rest of our stuff. But the good news is I'm back with Hattie. If she's leaving, I'm leaving, too.

My chest heaves with excitement as Hattie clips the leash to my collar. Fetch Man and Food Lady head for the door, lugging suitcases. I pull Hattie after them, down the hall and into the elevator. Where we go all . . . the way . . . down to the bottom. *Ding!*

When we get to the car, Hattie opens the door. I shoot inside before anybody can stop me. I lick Hattie's cheek. It's wet and salty. "It's all right. I'm here to protect you," I bark. "Nothing can go wrong now."

We zoom along for a Long, Long Time. I climb higher on Hattie's chest and poke my head out the window. We're on a road that's slower and bumpier. With trees that are leafier, smells that are flowerier, and air that is breezier.

We pull into a grassy park and stop. As the car goes quiet, Fetch Man smiles and squeezes Food Lady's hand.

My paws are all over the window. "Somebody let me out!"

Hattie grabs my leash, and we burst out of the car. I bury my nose in the cool, refreshing grass. It smells of wild animals. Like squirrels, chipmunks, mysterious birds . . . and not one single pigeon.

I raise my head, my ears perked and listening. But I don't hear any traffic rumbling or honking or snorting. Or music drifting from cars or stores. All I hear are birds chirping and squirrels chattering. A motor buzzes in the distance. Short humans squeal somewhere down the street. What is this place?

Fetch Man and Food Lady hurry up a walkway that leads to a house. They're acting awfully excited, like it's the most wonderful house they've ever seen.

Hattie yanks me out of the grass mid-pee, and we follow along up the front steps. She must be eager to check out the house, too.

Oh boy! Whatever's inside must be really amazing. Like a pile of bones! Or a slab of meat!

Fetch Man opens the door and we all race in, full of anticipation. Hooray! Hooray! I can hardly wait!

I run a few circles around Hattie's legs as she unclips the leash. "Hurry, Hattie!" I bark. I have to find out what's so special.

I search around, but all I see is a big empty space. And it smells totally boring, like stale air and fresh paint and new carpeting. It must get better, right?

I start out trotting with my nose to the ground. Pretty soon, I'm sprinting down the hall on a Perfect Running Surface that I wish would go on forever. But then I make a sharp turn and cruise into a bright and gleaming place where the floor feels different. Smoother. And slipperier.

Suddenly, the floor gives way. My paws lose their grip and—whoa!—I'm skidding and skidding, my legs scrambling out of control. And then—*smack!* I'm crumpled up against a tall and shiny box that's humming. *Ouch!* What happened?

Hattie appears. "Fenway!" she cries, her voice sounding worried. She stoops next to me. She rubs my head and coos softly in my ear.

Food Lady rushes in and crouches next to us. She lifts my paws one by one, inspecting them like she's looking for fleas.

I glance down and growl at the Wicked Floor. Talk about a sneak attack. I never saw it coming.

My defeat is so embarrassing. I can't even look at Hattie or Food Lady. Instead, I gaze around the room. It reminds me of our Eating Place at home. Only much,

much bigger. And emptier. And worst of all, it does not smell anything like an Eating Place should. It smells really bad. Like soap.

Which can only mean one thing—no food.

Food Lady gives me a quick rub, then abruptly goes to the counter. She starts opening drawers. She must be searching for nothing. Because that's what she's finding, and she's acting rather happy about it.

Hattie continues stroking my back and kissing my neck. At least my short human understands how serious the problem is. She wraps her arms around me and rests her head on my back.

Fetch Man comes striding in like he owns the place. Hey! How are the humans moving around so easily? Does the Wicked Floor only terrorize dogs? Fetch Man sidles up next to Food Lady and wraps his arms around her waist. She tells him something, and he steps away, looking concerned.

He turns to me, his face full of surprise. Like he just realized the pathetic heap in the corner is actually a dog. He comes over and gives me a pat. "Okay, fella?"

He swoops Hattie into his arms and lifts her up into the air. She explodes into a fit of giggles.

How can they have fun at a time like this?

Well, I know one thing—I'm not about to sit around

waiting for the Wicked Floor to strike again. But how to get away? I need an idea, but it's hard to think when my tail is sagging and my ears are drooping. I gaze back at my humans, who are clearly busy with other things. Fetch Man is hugging Hattie like crazy, and Food Lady is at the stove turning the knobs, even though there's no food to cook.

With no brilliant ideas and no help on the horizon, I try moving and barely manage to stand up. I clench my claws and take one step. Whoa! My legs slip out from under me again.

I get back up, panting like a coward. I tense my whole body and try again . . . then—*ooof!* I'm splat back down on that glossy, sinister surface.

It is pure evil.

I can't just lie here. I must find a way to escape. I try again and again, slipping and scrambling the whole long way. But finally, I make it through the doorway and onto the safety of the carpet. Whew!

Back in the hall, it's all I can do to catch my breath. Thank goodness that's over. But right then, Fetch Man glances over and evidently decides it's playtime.

He gives Hattie a long look. He squats down and slaps his leg. "Fenn-waay," he calls, his eyes staring at me, wide and bright. What's wrong with him? Does he think I've already forgotten about the Wicked Floor?

There must be somewhere I can hide. I turn tail and race around the corner. I discover steps that go up so high, I can't see where they end. But they probably end somewhere, and anywhere is better than the Eating Place with that Wicked Floor. In a flash, I'm all the way at the top.

And somebody is right behind me. It's Hattie! I know that devilish sound of her footsteps. She wants to play chase, our favorite game! "Ha, you can't catch me, Hattie," I bark. I turn and take off back down the steps as fast as I can. Hattie loves chase so much, sometimes I let her win. But this is not one of those times.

Whew! I'm panting hard when I get to the bottom. But when I steal a look up over my shoulder . . . where is Hattie?

I must go search for her. I scamper back up, step after step after step. My tongue hanging out, my sides heaving, at last I make it all the way to the top. "Hattie! Hattie!" I bark. I sure could use some water.

But first things first. I need to find Hattie! Nose to the carpet, I follow her minty-vanilla trail down another hallway. This one has doors. One room, another, and another . . . and they're all enormous. And empty.

Except the last room is not empty—Hattie's inside! She's at the window. Is she looking for something outside?

"Hooray! Hooray!" I bark, rushing in. "I found you!"

"Fenn-waay!" She turns and bends down. She scoops me into her arms. "Best buddies," she sings, snuggling my fur.

I lick her chin.

We twirl around the huge empty room. Hattie stretches out an arm, like she wants me to see how wonderful it is.

Um, okay. It doesn't smell interesting at all. And there's absolutely nothing in it. Not even one single toy.

Hattie hugs me tighter, swaying and dancing. Why is she so happy?

Just then ding-dong sounds float up from downstairs.

A doorbell! I squirt out of Hattie's arms. We run through the hall and down the stairs. "Someone's here! Someone's here!" I bark.

Fetch Man and Food Lady are already at the front door. And a Loud Truck is outside!

Despite my very vocal warnings, Fetch Man lets some Large Strangers stroll right in. They're carrying big boxes. And they reek of coffee and sweat, just like—hey! It's those same Evil Humans who stole our stuff!

Fetch Man welcomes them in like they belong here. Food Lady bosses them around the empty rooms.

"Go away! There's nothing here to steal," I snarl. "You already took it!"

But instead of appreciating my hard work, Fetch Man smells annoyed. He pulls me farther from the door. As usual, he doesn't get it. "Hattie," he scolds.

What? Does he actually think she's the one at fault here?

"Fenn-waay," Hattie sings in a playful voice, like nothing dangerous is happening. She snatches me up into her arms.

"Let me handle this," I bark, thrashing, desperate to get free. "I'm a professional."

But she holds me tighter and breezes to the back of the house. As she opens a sliding door, I can hardly believe my eyes.

@HapteR 3

Hattie lets out a little shriek, like she's
surprised, too. Right behind the house is an open space
with grass and a giant tree near the back. Clusters of
bushes and a fence run along all the sides. My tail goes
berserk. It can only be one thing—a Dog Park!

But it's kind of plain. Where is the big water dish to
splash in? Or the benches to jump on?

And it's quiet. Too quiet. I turn my snout into the
breeze, but all I catch are whiffs of leaves and grass and
blooming flowers. Where are the romping dogs? Are we
the first to arrive?

I look back at the door. Where is Fetch Man? Who's
going to throw the ball for me and Hattie to chase?

This place is curious, all right. But one thing's for
sure—it must be explored!

I wiggle out of Hattie's arms and drop onto the porch. She chases me down the steps. Yippee! It's time to play!

I tear around the Dog Park, zigging and zagging. If Hattie wants to catch me, she's going to have to outrace the master!

But as I make a sharp turn, Hattie's not behind me. She's in the middle of the Dog Park, somersaulting through the grass. Is this a new game? I hustle over and slobber her face with licks.

She flops onto her back, laughing. I sink down next to her and nuzzle her chin. "Come on, Hattie! It's play-time," I bark.

She closes her eyes and hums. She must be too comfortable to get up.

It's obvious she's going to need some convincing. And I know just how to do it!

Nose in the grass, I trot off in search of a stick. I haven't gotten far when I start to realize something. I haven't sniffed any messages from other dogs. How strange!

I stop to leave one or two, so new dogs will know I'm here and ready to play. Right as I'm watering a strategic spot, I get sidetracked by a horrible rodent-y smell. A squirrel!

I look over and spot his fat, nasty body up ahead.

He's sitting proudly in the Dog Park, his tail flounced up like he deserves to be here.

My own tail shoots up. I race over to show him who's boss.

But he's not acting the least bit intimidated. He just sits there in the grass, glaring at me. Does he think I'm not serious?

I bare my teeth. I'm ready to pounce! I'm about to grab his squirrel-y fur when suddenly, he pivots and rockets toward the back fence. I'm hot on his tail. "A Dog Park is for dogs!" I bark after him.

He scurries partway up the trunk of the giant tree, then pauses to flick his bushy tail at me. *"Chipper, chatter, squawk!"* he screeches, daring me to nab him.

I spring up, furiously pawing the tree, but he's just out of reach. "You coward!" I bark. I run in circles around the giant tree, every hackle on my back raised in alarm.

The squirrel turns and creeps down the trunk, tantalizingly close. *"Chipper, chatter, squawk!"* he screeches again.

I leap and leap, scraping the bark with my claws. "It's called a DOG Park for a reason!" I growl.

But instead of scampering away, he inches closer. His beady eyes are challenging me.

Does he not know who he's dealing with? I jump higher and higher, my jaws ready to snap!

Finally, he gets the message. He scrambles way up the trunk.

I watch until he disappears in the rustling and swaying branches. I'm about to bark "Good riddance!" when I spot his flouncy tail shooting through . . . a window?

I leap back, straining for a better view. There, up in the giant tree, nestled in the leafy leaves, is a little house about as tall as Hattie. A squirrel's nest that looks like a little house? Whoa! The squirrels around here are even more evil than the ones at home.

At least that nasty squirrel's up in the tree where he belongs. "Wait till next time, you pest!" I bark with one last snarl.

Wow, that was a lot of hard work!

I turn to get Hattie, but she's already headed over. Whoopee! I know that look in her eyes—she's ready to play!

I snatch the nearest stick and gallop straight toward her. But at the last second, she darts out of the way. Ha! The chase is on!

I'm speeding along near the side fence when I hear a sound that stops me in my tracks. *Clink! Jingle! Jingle!*

Hooray! Hooray! More dogs are coming! I peer through the slats.

I can hardly believe what I see. Two dogs—in another Dog Park. Two Dog Parks, side by side? They must notice me, too, because the Golden Retriever stops chasing her tail and lopes over. The other dog does, too.

Their noses sniff wildly, examining me as best they can through the fence. The smaller one's mostly white like me, only with black patches.

Being checked out by a couple of ladies is not so bad, but after a while the silence can be kind of . . . humiliating.

I drop the stick. "Looks like an awesome Dog Park over there," I say. "Not sure if you know this, but there's another one right here."

The white one opens her mouth like she wants to say something, but the Golden speaks first. "A Dog Park?" she says, as if she cannot believe the news.

"Yes, two right next to each other. Isn't it funny? I don't think anybody knows about this one, though. I probably discovered it."

"Are you saying . . . ?" the Golden says. "I mean, do you actually think you discovered—"

"Give him a chance, Goldie," the white one says in a gentle voice. She turns to me. "So, young fella, you're not from around here, are you?"

"Well, actually no, but—Goldie?" I glance from one dog to the other. "Did you call her Goldie? What an amazing coincidence. My humans used to have a gold-fish with that name."

"Excuse me?" The Golden gets all growly. "Are you comparing me to a fish?"

"No, never. I wouldn't do that." I slink back and turn to the second dog. She's not nearly as big as Goldie, but she's still a lot bigger than me.

"Of course you wouldn't," says the white dog. Even through the fence, I can smell how friendly she is. "Don't mind her. By the way, I'm Patches."

Patches. What a pretty name. And her voice sure is lovely.

Goldie shoots her a stern look.

"Why don't you tell us about yourself, young guy?" Patches says.

"Okay. My name's Fenway. I live in an apartment, way up high. Above the honking cars and snorting buses. Right next to the sidewalk that leads to the real Dog Park. Do you know it?"

Patches cocks her head, like she's not sure she heard me right. "Um, no . . ."

"Well, it's a really cool place. You'll just have to trust me."

Goldie nudges her. "We'd better listen to this guy," she says. "He sounds like he knows what he's talking about."

"Uh, so, anyway," I say. "This awesome Dog Park

won't be a secret for long. Why don't you ladies come try it out?"

Goldie and Patches exchange looks like they're not sure.

"You really should," I say. "Me and my short human came here to play. Why don't you join in? It's going to be amazing."

Goldie drops down and scratches. "Are you sure about that?"

"Look, I don't want to brag or anything. But Hattie's the best short human ever. She loves to play with me. And even though we're super best friends and we do everything together, you can play, too."

"You do everything together, huh?" Goldie says. "Does that include climbing trees?"

"Climbing trees? Right. That's a good one. What do you think we are, squirrels?"

Patches glances at the giant tree. "Um, I don't know how to tell you this . . ."

"Tell me what?"

"Fenn-waay!" calls a singsongy voice way above our heads. Hattie's voice. But how could it be? Why would her voice be up in the sky?

I crane my neck, but I don't see her. I scout around the Dog Park. Where did she go? "Hattie?" I bark.

"Fenn-waay!" floats down again. From the giant tree?

I look way up into the leafy branches. There, in the little squirrel house . . . a face is peering out the window . . . an arm is waving . . . It looks like Hattie. It sounds like Hattie. But Hattie doesn't climb trees. How did she get up there?

"Fenn-waay! Fenn-waay!" she calls, like maybe I didn't hear her the first bunch of times.

"Hattie!" I bark, running over. "What are you doing up there?"

She keeps on smiling and waving. Like she's perfectly happy up there in that squirrel house.

This is not right.

"Come down! Come down!" I bark again and again.

Hattie leans out the window, her arms resting on the ledge. Gazing down at me. Knowing I can't climb up and join her.

I turn away with a shudder. It's all so . . . squirrel-y.

"She loves to play with you, all right," Goldie says.

"Then what's she doing up in that tree? Don't tell me she expects you to follow her up there."

"Hey, now," Patches scolds. "It sounds like she's really into the guy."

"Humph," Goldie mutters.

"You never know," Patches says. "She could be back down here playing with him any second."

But she isn't. I sink into the grass. Why did we come here? Dog Parks are supposed to be for playing. Hattie is up in the giant tree, and the other dogs are not coming in. None of it makes sense.

I bury my face in my paws. When are we going home?

CHAPTER 4

I lie in the Dog Park for a Very Long Time.
At some point, a Lady Human's voice hollers for Goldie
and Patches. "See you around, Fenway," I hear Patches
say. I don't even respond.

Finally, my ears detect a Loud Truck roaring to life,
then zooming away. The sliding door opens, and Food
Lady appears. She has a puzzled look on her face. Her
head swivels. "Hattie?" she calls.

Rustling noises float down from the leafy branches,
and then . . . it's Hattie! She's climbing back down the
giant tree, the way Fetch Man does when he's coming
down a ladder. For the first time, I notice slats of wood
stuck to the far side of the trunk. When my short human's almost to the bottom, I jump up.

29

"Hattie!" I bark, leaping on her legs. "Is it playtime now?"

Apparently not. She scurries right past me to the porch, where Food Lady is standing. I race up behind her.

But as soon as we're through the door, something is different. The house is not empty anymore. I cruise into the big room in the front. It's filled with scents that I recognize right away—Fetch Man's socks and newspaper and potato chips—just like our Lounging Place at home. There's even a couch that smells exactly like the one Food Lady won't let me climb on. How did it get here?

I poke my head into another room and find Fetch Man busy opening boxes. I zoom down the hall and peer into the Eating Place. Food Lady is busy opening boxes, too. Where is Hattie?

I follow her scent over to the high staircase. I bound all the way to the top and tear down the hall into the room where she was before.

There she is! Hattie's also taking things out of boxes—clothes and shoes and toys. She must be very busy, because when I enter, she doesn't even look up. I vault onto a bed that wasn't there before. It smells minty and vanilla-ish like Hattie's bed. I curl up into a ball and close my eyes.

Next thing I know, an alarming sound from downstairs wakes me up.

Ding-dong! Ding-dong!

The doorbell!

I hear Fetch Man's voice, then the noise of the front door closing. Intruders again? I shoot off the bed and fly down the stairs past Hattie.

The instant my paws hit the bottom step, a delicious scent fills my nose. It smells like gooey cheese, yummy sauce, and spicy pepperoni. It can only be one thing—pizza!

Yippee! I love pizza! I knew something wonderful was happening. "Great news, Hattie. Pizza!" I bark as we rush down the hall.

But when she heads inside the Eating Place, I hang back on the safety of the carpet. I poke my snout through the doorway and inhale the luxuriously spicy and savory aroma. My tongue drips uncontrollably.

Hattie and Fetch Man are sitting at a table, just like the one in our Eating Place at home. Food Lady opens a thin box and puts steaming slices of pizza on paper plates.

I want to dash right in and wait for yummy bits of sauce and gooey strings of cheese to drop from Hattie's spot. But unfortunately, there's a Very Big Problem.

The Wicked Floor.

That pizza smells so pizza-y. And my tummy is so hungry. There must be a way to get over to Hattie and plop next to her chair.

I put one paw on the Wicked Floor's glossy, sinister surface. Yikes! It slides out from under me. Clearly, I'm no match for this monster.

I slither back onto the carpet and collapse in a heap. I peer through the doorway, defeated. And drooling.

"Fenn-waay," Hattie calls, like she just realized somebody was missing. Clearly, my short human is unaware of the evil lurking beneath her feet. She gazes at me with sad eyes. "Awww." Her voice is filled with pity.

"Can't we eat pizza out here in the hallway?" I whine.

Hattie looks like she'd be up for it. But Food Lady has other ideas. She gets up and heads over to one of the big boxes. She pulls out a dish that looks just like mine. My tummy starts to rumble.

Food Lady grabs a lumpy bag that I recognize right away. I immediately start panting. She takes out a scoop, and the exciting sound of dog food rattles right on in.

Wowee! It's supper time!

I spring to my feet, my tongue slurping in tasty anticipation. "I'm so ready! I'm so ready!" I bark.

But just like that, the happy scene turns terrible once

more. Food Lady places my dish right on the Wicked Floor, then goes back to her seat. She nods at Hattie.

"Fenn-waay," Hattie calls, her face hopeful. She points at my bowl as if I might not have noticed it.

Why is she doing this?

"Fenn-waay," she calls again. But nothing has changed. My dish is still on the Wicked Floor. Why is Hattie torturing me?

I crumple onto the carpet, my tummy growling. Food Lady and Fetch Man are patting Hattie's arm, like they're comforting her. Hey, I'm the one who needs comforting, people!

There must be a way to get that food.

Hattie goes back to eating her pizza, but she keeps sneaking sorry looks at me. And then, in a flash, I know what to do.

I push myself up and stretch my head inside the doorway. I put on my most pathetic face. "Stop torment-ing me," I whine. I move up to the edge of the Wicked Floor. I whimper some more.

Hattie tilts her head to the side. She looks like her heart is breaking.

I fall to my belly, paws stretched out in front. I whine longer and louder. "You know you want to help me, Hat-tie. You don't want me to starve, do you?"

I can tell from her eyes that she's starting to cave. I give it everything I've got.

"Oh please, oh please, Hattie," I moan. "I'm sooooooooooo hungry!"

It works! Hattie leaps out of her seat and snatches my dish off the Wicked Floor. While Fetch Man and Food Lady look on disapprovingly, she carries it out into the hallway.

Before she even sets it down—*chomp! Mmmmm!* Wow, is it scrumptious.

For the next few seconds, I'm lost in a crunchy, munchy world of Pure Deliciousness. Until all too soon, the bowl is empty.

I let out a burp of deep satisfaction. That's my short human! I knew she'd come through.

When the windows are dark, I'm upstairs in Hattie's room, lounging on the bed. I sprawl out on the cozy blanket, ready for my bedtime brushing.

Hattie appears smelling strongly of mint, same as every night. She kisses my brown paw, my white paw, then showers my neck with kisses.

I give her cheek a slobbery lick, and she giggles.

She grabs the hairbrush, snuggling next to me and singing in her sweet voice. "Best buddies, best buddies."

Aaaaah! Each soothing stroke transforms my body into complete and total bliss. I roll over for the other side as Hattie keeps on brushing and singing away. When she gets to my belly, my hind leg kicks with delight.

As the room grows darker and darker, my eyelids get heavy. I close them just for a second and then . . .

I'm outside by the giant tree. And what's that horrible smell? It's so . . . squirrel-ish.

There he is! That fat, nasty squirrel is sitting in the middle of the Dog Park again. Except now he's even fatter and nastier than before. His belly is bigger than my whole body! And his teeth are sharp, drooly fangs!

Yikes!

I search for cover behind the nearest bush, but it's too late. He's spotted me.

"Chipper, chatter, squawk!" he screeches, waving his massive, fluffy tail and scampering toward me at full speed.

"Get out of here . . . you . . . p-p-pest," I bark in my fiercest voice.

But apparently, he doesn't hear. He's hurtling straight at me when suddenly—

Crrrrrack! Boom! Kaboom!

Whoa, that's one loud squirrel! My eyelids pop open. Hey—he's gone. And I'm back in Hattie's soft, cozy bed.

A bright light flashes. Rain pounds against the window. Oh no, there's a storm outside! With boom-kabooms!

Hattie bolts up, her eyes wide. She clutches the used-to-be bear.

Shaking with courage, I crawl onto her chest. I nuzzle the used-to-be bear. Hattie pats my back. "Best buddies," she whispers.

I sigh with happiness. Me and Hattie are together, and everything's the way it's supposed to be. We are home.

Chapter 5

When it's morning time outside, the door-
bell sounds again. Intruders!

"Watch out!" I bark, rushing over. "A vicious dog is
on patrol!"

Despite the very obvious risk of danger, Fetch Man
opens the front door.

A Lady Human is standing on the porch. Next to her
is a short human about the same size as Hattie. She is
wearing a cap exactly like Fetch Man's, only hers has a
long wavy tail hanging out the back.

"Hel-lo," the Lady Human sings. She's holding a basket that smells like warm muffins. With cinnamon!

"Wowee!" I bark, running in circles. "Muffins! Muffins! I love muffins!"

Muffin Lady laughs a friendly laugh and talks for a bit. "Nay-ber," I hear her say.

Food Lady hurries over, full of happy chatter. I hear her say, "Nay-ber," too. She welcomes them inside.

I jump on their legs, sniffing furiously. The short human smells amazing, like bubble gum and Fetch Man's fat leather glove and . . . dogs! Golden Retriever and another breed I can't quite identify. Muffin Lady smells even more strongly of dogs. Familiar dogs . . .

Food Lady is smiling at Muffin Lady like she's her best friend. Did I mention she's carrying a basket of muffins?

And they smell so warm and cinnamony! I leap higher and higher, my paw batting her knee.

Muffin Lady startles, but sadly, not even one muffin spills out of the basket.

"FEN-way," Fetch Man scolds. He turns to Muffin Lady, shrugging sheepishly. "Puppy," I hear him say.

Muffin Lady laughs again and says, "Ram-bunk-shuss." That must mean she likes me, because she stoops down and scratches behind my ears.

My humans are wincing in horror. What do they have against a dog making new friends? Food Lady snatches the basket and wraps it in her arms like she's trying to protect it. Fetch Man rushes to the stairs and calls for Hattie.

Why didn't I think of that? "Hattie! Hattie!" I race over. "Great news—muffins!"

Hattie arrives and steps into the Lounging Place. I trot along behind her, my tail swishing wildly.

Fetch Man puts his hand on her shoulder. "Hattie," he announces.

Muffin Lady grins and taps the cap of the other short human. "Angel," she says.

Angel glances at Hattie. She mutters something like a greeting, then her gaze drops to her feet.

Hattie edges closer, smiling and hopeful. But when Angel does not look up, Hattie smells disappointed.

Next thing I know, Food Lady herds everyone down the Perfect Running Surface and into the Eating Place. Except me.

I slump down on the carpet outside the doorway. The humans gather around the table. Pretty soon, they're all chattering, having a good time, and munching on those muffins. The warm scent of cinnamon taunts my nostrils. My eyes spot lovely crumbles near Hattie's feet. My belly aches.

"I'm hungry, too, you know," I whine, looking at them with sad eyes. "And I sure do looooove muffins."

Muffin Lady and Angel glance over with puzzled faces, like they've never seen a starving dog before.

Hattie grabs a muffin and starts to get up. Here it comes! I spring up in happy anticipation. I slurp my chops.

But Muffin Lady holds out her arm, and Hattie sits back down. "Train-ing?" Muffin Lady asks.

Food Lady and Fetch Man look embarrassed. Fetch Man shrugs. "Too-bizz-ee," Food Lady says.

What could it mean? It can't be good, because Hattie has clearly given up on bringing me that muffin. Instead, she stares straight at me and leans out over her knees. "Fenn-waay," she calls in a sweet voice.

Whoa, is she nuts? Does she actually think I'm going to run onto that Wicked Floor? I slink back down and lower my head, my gaze firmly on my short human.

Muffin Lady pats Hattie's arm and nods in approval.

Hattie holds out a chunk of muffin. "Fenn-waay," she calls, even sweeter this time.

That muffin looks so yummy. I sink down deeper into the cushy carpeting, my tummy empty and rumbling. This is not how My Hattie behaves. She's supposed to bring it to me.

It's all so horrible. Plus, they're having fun without me. There must be something I can do.

I get up and wander around, trying to think. And

before I know it, I'm at the sliding door. Aha! Why didn't I think of it sooner? "Hurry! Hurry!" I wail, jumping up and scratching the screen. "Somebody let me out. Right now!"

It works! Hattie and Angel appear at my side. They open the door, and we all zoom through.

The short humans blast down the steps, and I'm right behind them. I'm ready for fun!

The grass is wet and puddle-y. Still no signs of other dogs, but it could be worse—at least there are no squirrels.

Hattie and Angel have a head start, but I'm up for the chase. I'm hot on their heels as they run through the grass. Of course, I'd rather be chased than be the chaser, but sometimes it's okay to mix things up.

But when Hattie and Angel get to the giant tree, they stop. I get a bad feeling. Hattie points at the way-up-high leafy branches. She shows Angel the ladder-y steps on the back of the trunk.

As I'm barreling over, Hattie starts climbing. "Come on," she says.

Angel smiles, but she smells hesitant.

I leap up, pawing the bottom rung. "No fair, Hattie," I bark. "We can't play chase up there."

"Come on," Hattie says again from halfway up the trunk.

She's obviously heading for that little squirrel house again. I collapse into the soggy grass with a groan.

Angel sighs, then begins climbing up after Hattie.

I'm still watching long after the short humans disappear into the leafy leaves.

I'm about to go sniff around some more, but then my ears perk to wonderful jingly sounds. Hooray! Hooray! Dogs are coming!

I get up and trot over to the fence. Through the slats, I see two of them romping around in the Dog Park next door. "Um, hey . . . hello," I call.

The dogs stop mid-romp and gallop over. "Fenway?" says the white one in her lovely voice.

"I told you he'd be back," says the Golden.

Sure enough, it's those same two ladies. Are they the only two visitors to that Dog Park? And why don't they come to this one? "Great memory," I say. "So, uh, have you two been coming here for always?"

They exchange glances, then look back at me. "What do you mean? We live here," Goldie says.

I cock my head. "You live in a Dog Park?"

Goldie gets an irritated look and opens her mouth. But before she can answer, Patches says, "Was that our short human you were trying to chase just now?"

"What? No, it was mine. Hattie, remember?"

"Oh, we remember," Goldie says with a growl. "How

did you say it, super best friends? You do everything together. Isn't that right?"

Patches rolls her eyes at Goldie, then turns back to me. "I meant Angel."

"Wow, she's your short human?" No wonder she smelled like Golden Retriever and . . . whatever kind of dog Patches is.

"Well, she used to be," Goldie says.

I look at her sideways. "Isn't she still?"

"Technically, yes. But things change." Patches lowers her head. "In the beginning, she was fun, a lot like your Hattie. We'd walk to the river and play fetch—"

"I believe it was the pond and we played Frisbee," Goldie corrects.

"Fact is," Patches says, a faraway gleam in her eye, "she used to be great. I thought she would always stay that way."

Goldie scowls. "I knew it wouldn't last."

"As I recall, you were awfully fond of her," Patches says. "We both were."

"She had a lot of potential. Like most short humans," Goldie says.

"It's so tragic," Patches says. "Short humans never stay interested in anything for very long."

"Sad, but true." Goldie huffs. "They go from one thing to another. Without even looking back."

"Nowadays, she acts like we're not even here," Patches says, a little yelp in her voice.

Goldie paws the ground. "She's totally forgotten about the good times we used to have . . ."

"Gee, that's such a bummer for you," I say. "But not all short humans are like that. Hattie's different."

Goldie snorts. "Are you sure about that?"

"You don't know her. She's completely devoted to me," I insist. "She's the best short human ever."

"Maybe that's how it was *before*," Goldie says, drawing out the last word. "But it doesn't look that way now."

"What are you talking about?" I say, but when I gaze up into the giant tree, I have my answer. Hattie's smiling face is poking out of the squirrel-house window. Without me. And a massive boulder crushes my heart.

CHAPTER 6

Hattie and Angel stay up in the squirrel house for a Long, Long Time. I curl up in the cool grass while Goldie and Patches wander away, muttering to each other.

I wait and wait. Until finally, the leafy leaves whoosh, the branches sway, and two pairs of feet are scaling down the giant tree.

Yippee! I leap as high as I can, pawing furiously at the bottom rung. "That's my short human!" I bark. "I knew you'd come back."

Hattie reaches the ladder-y step just above my head, then jumps. "Wheeeee!" she shouts, landing in the grass with a giggle.

Angel looks like she wants to jump, too, but changes

45

her mind. She continues climbing down as I'm spring-ing up.

My brown paw swipes Angel's calf, and somehow she loses her footing. "Oh no!" she wails.

I back away as she falls, landing—*splat!*—on the ground.

Hattie rushes to Angel's side, her face full of concern.

"Owwwww!" Angel cries. She rubs her bum, scowl-ing at me. She gets to her feet and dusts off her clothes. "All-rite," she says to Hattie.

Hattie looks relieved. Next thing I know, the short humans are heading for the back porch.

I bound after them. "Hey, wait for me!"

Angel punches her palm a couple of times. "Ball?" she asks. Her long, wavy hair hangs out the back of her cap like a squirrel's tail.

Hattie shakes her head. "Jump-rope?" she says.

Angel scrunches up her face. "Nah," she says. She pauses for a moment, her gaze wandering. Then her shoulders sink and she disappears through the door.

Hattie sighs. She smells disappointed.

"Don't feel bad, Hattie," I bark, dancing around her feet. "We're in the Dog Park. It's time to play!" I shoot out into the grass.

But instead of chasing me, Hattie trudges right on by.

"Try to catch me!" I bark, zooming along ahead of her. Straight to the giant tree.

Hattie grabs onto a high rung and starts climbing.

I watch until her feet disappear, my tail drooping. I sink back down. My Hattie does not belong in a tree. My Hattie belongs down here in the grass, chasing me. Or scooping me into her arms and showering me with kisses. Laughing, having the time of her life. Protesting when Fetch Man makes us leave the Dog Park to go home. That's My Hattie.

But this Hattie is up in that giant tree again. Does she really want to hang out with those nasty squirrels? With no loyal dog to keep her safe? And protect her from grave danger? What if something bad happens to her?

Hey, wait a minute—that's it! I run in circles. I know how to get My Hattie back!

After all, I'm a professional. I'll save her from dangerous squirrels! And Evil Humans! Why didn't I think of it sooner? It's the Best Idea Ever!

She'll remember how important I am, and she'll change back to how she was before. She'll be My Hattie again. Like she's supposed to be. I spin and spin, every hair on my body itching to get to work. I'll be on guard for the right opportunity. It's only a matter of time.

The next day, I follow Hattie around the house. When danger strikes, I'll be ready.

Hattie fishes the long jump rope out of her backpack. She zooms into the Bathtub Room, where Food Lady is hanging a wide curtain. Hattie holds out the jump rope. "Please?" she begs.

Food Lady sighs and shakes her head.

Hattie's shoulders slump.

We hop down the stairs. Fetch Man is in the Lounging Place banging on the wall. When Hattie calls out to him, he turns around.

She shows him the jump rope. "Please?" she begs.

Fetch Man sighs, too. He puts a hand on Hattie's shoulder. He speaks to her in a gentle, hopeful voice. I catch one word.

"Angel?"

Hattie grimaces. She smells discouraged.

I know how she feels. So far nothing around here looks or smells the least bit dangerous. I'm starting to think my plan to save her isn't going to work when that terrifying sound comes from the front door again.

Ding-dong!

I spring into action. "Warning! Warning!" I bark,

bravely rushing to the source of the danger. "Nobody go near that door."

Fetch Man heads right toward it like he doesn't even hear me.

"Watch out!" I bark. "It's probably a grave threat to our safety—"

Aha! A grave threat! This is my big chance to save Hattie.

I hurry over to her. "Bad news! We're all in jeopardy! Stay where you are. I'll protect you."

I race back to Fetch Man, growling and snarling. Totally ignoring me, he opens the door like nothing is wrong. "Stand back!" I bark. "I can handle this. I'm a professional."

And sure enough, standing in front of us is an Evil Human wearing a hard hat on his head and dirty boots on his feet. He's carrying a bag that's heavy and bulging. One whiff reveals German Shepherd and telephone poles and a hint of ham sandwich. With mustard.

And that's not all. He's whistling—a sure sign of trouble!

Fetch Man greets the Evil Human with a cheery voice, like he's happy to see him. He invites him right in, completely unfazed by my growls. "Be forewarned!"

49

I bark at the intruder. "Don't take one step toward that short human over by the couch!"

The Evil Human breezes right by, as if he's not even the least bit intimidated. He strolls into the Lounging Place, straight toward Hattie. Fetch Man and I follow. He's gritting his teeth. I'm baring mine. I'm ready to nip at some heels if it comes to that.

At the Flashing Screen wall, the Evil Human stops. He stares at it for a second, even though it's black and not flashing. He squats down and opens his bag. He takes out snaky wires and . . . scary tools!

I knew there'd be trouble! "Stop right there, buddy!" I bark, flinging myself at his leg. "There'll be none of those loud noises while I'm around."

Fetch Man crosses his arms. "Hattie," he snaps as she rushes over, right into the path of danger. Hey, Fetch Man is sabotaging my plan!

Or is he? "Get out of the way, Hattie! I've got this," I bark, thrusting out my chest. "This is no place for a short human."

Just then, a hand reaches down and rubs my head. "Fella," says a strange but friendly voice.

The Evil Human! What is he trying to do? Throw me off my game?

"Fenn-waay! Fenn-waay!" Hattie says, backing away and clapping. She clearly wants to play.

"Not now, Hattie," I bark. "Can't you see how busy I am?"

She claps louder. "FEN-way," Hattie says. This time, she sounds annoyed.

What's going on? This is not part of the plan. "Hattie, I'm trying to protect you from this Evil Human who has invaded our home," I bark, and—whoa!

The menace revs up the roaring tool!

I lunge toward his arm, stopping a safe distance from the earsplitting sound. "Put that thing down before somebody gets hurt!"

Hattie's hands close around my torso. "FEN-way!" she cries.

"Cut it out, Hattie," I bark as she lifts me up and away from the Evil Human. "I'm supposed to be the one saving you!"

And that's not the only problem. Hattie smells different. Frustrated. She mutters something to Fetch Man over her shoulder. She carries me out of the Lounging Place. Why isn't she happy that her loyal dog is trying to protect her?

She keeps on walking to the sliding door. When she opens it, I finally realize what's going on. We're going outside to the Dog Park!

She sets me down on the porch and gazes into my eyes. She points her finger at me. "Fenway," she says, her voice serious. There is something important she wants me to know. Probably that she's completely devoted to me and nothing will ever come between us.

And it hits me—my plan worked! We're going to play, same as always. Hooray! Hooray! My Hattie's back!

But then, a terrible thing happens. She opens the door and goes back inside. Without me.

CHapter 7

Later, Food Lady's in the Eating Place with the promising sounds of running water, noisy pots, and scraping spoons. Delicious smells are drifting through the house. It's all I can do to slurp the drool from my muzzle.

Hattie and Fetch Man charge in and gather around the table. I'm parked in the safe hallway, looking through the door. And I see a wonderful sight—Food Lady's pouring tasty food into my dish! As it's rattling in, I jump up and run in circles. Yippee! It's supper time.

Food Lady sets my dish on the Wicked Floor. She takes her seat next to Hattie and Fetch Man. My tummy is rumbling. I smack my chops. I can hardly wait!

Hattie glances at Food Lady, then back at me. "Fenn-waay," she calls in a hopeful voice.

I know the routine by now. I cock my head and put on my most pathetic face. I whimper and moan, "Please, oh please, Hattie. I'm sooooo hungry . . ."

Hattie turns to Food Lady. She wants to bring me that dish.

"No," Food Lady says.

Fetch Man shakes his head. "Train-ing," he says.

What's wrong? Hattie's supposed to get up and serve me my food out here in the hallway.

I whine some more. "Hattie, Hattie, oh please, Hattie. Please, please, pleeeeeaaaaase . . ."

She's gazing at Fetch Man, then Food Lady, then back to Fetch Man. She looks desperate. She wants to help me. What's going on?

I cry and whimper and whine again and again and again. I even roll onto my back and moan, "Oh why, oh why isn't anybody feeding me? There's only so much suffering one dog can take."

It's hard work. I keep whining and moaning while my humans finish eating and put everything away. Hattie acts like it hurts to look at me. The feeling is mutual.

Just when I'm ready to give up, Hattie walks out of the Eating Place and over to the front closet. I spring up to see what's going on. She's holding her backpack and something even better—my leash. Good thing I showed up!

Fetch Man grabs jingling keys. Food Lady reaches for her purse. This can only mean one thing—we're going for a ride in the car! Whoopee!

Fetch Man and Food Lady are chattering up front. Me and Hattie are cuddled in the back. She speaks to me in a quiet voice, like she's telling me a secret. She pets me over and over.

My nose detects a fabulous scent in her backpack. There's no doubt about it! That thing is loaded with treats! Hattie's obviously planning to give them to me. I can't stop licking her face. This is the way it's supposed to be! My Hattie is back.

When the car stops, I barrel out the door, ready for all the fun we are about to have with those treats. And when I search around the parking lot, there's more excitement right in front of my eyes. And my nose! Lots of dogs and humans. And they're heading into a giant building.

An indoor Dog Park? Hooray! Hooray! I pull Hattie through the doors. I can't get in fast enough.

But inside, it's disturbingly quiet. And worse, the dogs are all on leashes. "What is this place?" I say as we approach a Yellow Lab.

After we politely sniff each other's bums, he tells me his name is Lance. He's with a tall human who smells like hamburger. "Dunno, dude," he says. "But then, I rarely do."

"Well, it's going to be wonderful," I say.

He gazes at me blankly. "Huh?"

I nuzzle Hattie's leg. "This is my short human. Her backpack is full of treats!"

He perks up. "Treats? Awesome!"

Food Lady and Fetch Man are speaking with some other humans. One of them is tugging the leash of a Basset Hound who looks like he wants to run away. Does he know something I don't? We introduce ourselves. His name is Rocky.

This place sure is curious. It must be explored! Nose to the floor, I lead Hattie from corner to corner, intoxicated by the amazing aromas. Every single inch of space smells like dogs. All kinds of dogs. I detect whiffs of Schnauzers and Boxers and Poodles and every other breed I can imagine. Even more than I've ever smelled before. Has every kind of dog in the world been here? Talk about a promising sign! This place is probably the best indoor Dog Park ever. Or maybe Dog Heaven.

As I continue to sniff, I discover something even more incredible—treats! And not just the delicious kind in Hattie's backpack. Wowee! It's a smorgasbord of dog treats—cheesy, livery, beefy—the smells are totally overwhelming. I pivot and jump on Hattie's legs. "This is going to be mind-blowing!" I bark. "I can hardly wait till the fun starts!"

She looks around uneasily and shifts her backpack to her other shoulder. She smells nervous. Why isn't she more excited? And more important, why isn't she handing over the treats?

Suddenly, I notice that One Human is striding toward us very purposefully. Like maybe she wants some treats, too. Well, she's going to have a fight on her hands.

Or maybe not. The One Human's energy is friendly, yet her posture is telling me to stay on guard. A bad combination.

She starts talking, and Hattie's treating her like she's Very Important. She says that mysterious word "train-ing," too.

Hattie grips the leash tighter, like she wants to keep her loyal dog close. There's something puzzling about this One Human. Besides the fact that she smells like the same wonderful combination of dogs and treats as everything else in this place.

All of a sudden, she turns and begins talking to everyone, like she's in charge. And the humans all fall for it. They go quiet, staring at her with rapt attention. The dogs, not so much.

Rocky digs his hind claws into the floor like he's being dragged into the vet's office.

The roundest Beagle I've ever seen turns to me with noticeable effort. "Did I hear something about treats?"

I bounce on my paws. "You bet!" I say. "Tons of them! I smelled them with my own nose."

"Good. I'm starving," she says. "But there better not be any work involved. I don't do work."

I gaze at her, bewildered. She tells me her name is Sadie.

The One Human keeps on talking, the humans keep on listening, and the dogs have no idea what's going on. Do the humans expect us to just hang out and wait patiently? It's the very definition of impossible.

All the dogs start barking at once. "I want to go home," Rocky howls.

Lance jumps on his human's legs, nearly knocking him over. "Where are the treats?" he barks.

"I hope I won't be expected to run around or hop over anything," says Sadie, sprawling out and yawning. "That's not how I roll."

"Hold on, you guys," I say. "I have a good feeling about this."

Rocky stops howling and eyes me with suspicion. "Who died and made you Alpha Dog?"

I sink down. "Nobody. I mean, let's give it a chance."

"A chance?" Sadie says, nodding at the anxious-smelling humans standing next to her. "Honey, it's obvious you haven't been around very long."

The One Human says a magical word we all know.

"Treats."

Every single ear perks up!

I spring up, my tail going nuts. "See?" I tell the others.

"It's about time," Sadie says, struggling to push herself onto all fours.

"Huh?" says Lance.

Sure enough, the humans produce treats. But for some reason everybody's focused on the One Human instead of the dogs.

The dogs begin jumping and sniffing at the closed fists. Given the totally unfair height advantage, the humans win. For now.

I turn to Hattie, who's clutching a handful of tasty little nuggets. Her face is glowing with excitement. "Ready?" she asks.

"I'm so ready! I'm so ready!" I bark, darting back and forth.

She leans over and holds out her fist. "Fenway, sit."

I leap up as high as I can, my nose going crazy. *Mmmmm!* Those treats are in there all right! The meaty fragrance is undeniable. I nip and nip, but Hattie's hand remains closed.

Why aren't those treats dropping into my mouth? Hattie's excited face is unchanged. She speaks again. "Ready, Fenway? Sit. Sit. Sit!"

"I'm so ready! I'm so ready!" I jump and jump, my

tail going berserk. Come on! Why aren't the treats coming?

Hattie's cheeks droop. So do her eyes.

Is this some kind of game? It isn't very fun. For either of us. Hattie seems almost as upset as I am.

Fetch Man puts his hand on Hattie's back. Food Lady nods at her reassuringly.

I'm about to ask why she's the one they're reassuring when our heads turn toward a commotion on the other side of the room. Lance is jumping and pawing his human. "Yo, buddy! Where are the treats?" he barks.

The One Human heads over to them. Lance's human steps aside, as if he expects the One Human to rescue him. He's grimacing like he's in pain. Or perhaps he's afraid of what's next. Lance turns to the rest of us. "What're you lookin' at?"

The One Human stands over Lance, stares straight into his eyes, and something changes. His face becomes completely focused. He gapes at the One Human like she's a ham bone. "Sit," she says.

He plunks onto his bum. And voilà! A treat falls into his open mouth. It's beyond impressive.

But it's not over. "Stay," the One Human says, holding out her arm. She steps back. Lance waits, completely still, eyes glued on her as if in a trance. Another treat sails over and—nice grab! This happens a few more times.

We're all thinking the same thing—it can't be that easy. But nobody has the guts to do anything about it. Or do they? I turn to Sadie, then to Rocky. "Just watch, you guys," I say. "I totally have this."

I swivel back to Hattie. "Yo, buddy! Where's my treat?" I bark. I jump up and paw her legs.

She jerks away. "FEN-way!"

I can feel rather than see the attention. "Come on. Where is it?" I bark again, charging at her.

Right on cue, the One Human comes over. One sniff reveals that she has treats, too. She hovers over me, her body tall and dominant.

"Sit," she commands.

Talk about intimidating! My hind legs crumple. I sink onto my bum.

She looks into my eyes. "Stay," she says, extending her arm.

I freeze in place. I want to hop up and grab those treats. But her strong gaze and powerful energy are warning me not to.

The One Human takes a step.

I'm still as a statue—work it, work it, work it—and bingo! *Chomp!* The treat's in my mouth, and wowee, is it ever yummy.

Really, this game is too easy. Apparently, the One Human's not very smart.

When it's dark outside, we're back at home. I'm curled up in Hattie's cozy bed. She's smelling minty. And subdued.

She quickly kisses my front paws, then begins brushing my fur. I sigh happily with each luxurious stroke. I snuggle against My Hattie's chest, ready to melt into a pool of delight.

But something's different. Instead of singing "best buddies, best buddies," she's talking. In that same quiet, serious voice she used before. She's telling me to pay attention to something important. But what?

CHAPTER 8

When it's morning time, Hattie rubs her eyes. Yippee, she's awake!

I crawl up to her face and lick her cheek, my whole backside wagging with excitement. "Get up, Hattie!" I bark. "It's time to play."

She laughs and strokes my back. Then she rolls over, her gaze drifting to the top of the dresser. Where her backpack is.

She gets out of bed and reaches for it. My tail goes crazy with a wonderful memory. That backpack is full of treats!

I fly off the bed, running around her bare feet. Hooray! Hooray! Treats are coming.

Hattie grabs a few treats and bounces on her toes. "Sit, Fenway!" she says.

Oh boy! I can't wait for those treats. I jump and jump, sniffing wildly at her fist. *Ouch!* I collide with the chair, and a stack of clean clothes tumbles to the floor.

As Hattie bends down to scoop them up, I'm ready. *Chomp! Mmmmm.* That was awfully easy. And tasty.

"FEN-way!" Hattie scolds, her voice annoyed.

What's up with that? Didn't she want me to have the treat?

Hattie sighs and starts refolding the clothes. Apparently, playtime is over. Or maybe not . . .

A bacon-y smell wafts in from the hallway. Wowee, I love bacon! I speed out the door. "Great news, Hattie!" I bark. "Bacon!"

I bound down the stairs, straight toward that bacon-y aroma. And sounds of popping and sizzling. Until I get to the Eating Place doorway and skid to a stop. My tummy sinks. Curse you, Wicked Floor!

Food Lady and Fetch Man are sitting at the table, holding steaming cups that smell like coffee. I inhale the smoky, salty scent of bacon. *Mmmmm!* My tongue can already taste it.

Hattie trots right on in, her energy full of purpose. She snatches a strip of glistening bacon and turns to me. "Fenway, come!" she says.

Fetch Man pats Food Lady's arm. His face is beaming with pride.

Hattie stretches out her hand, as if I didn't notice she was holding a piece of ripply, gorgeous bacon. "Fenway, come!" she says again.

My belly roars with desire. Saliva drips onto my whiskers. The Wicked Floor is standing between me and that—*gulp!*—wondrously yummy bacon.

Hattie gazes at me sweetly. She wants to give it to me. She edges closer. "Fenway, come!"

Why is she doing this to me? I jump up and up, scratching my claws against the wall. "Give me that bacon!" I whine.

Food Lady's eyes widen. Fetch Man shoots up from his seat.

"FEN-way, no!" Hattie shouts. She rushes over, shooing my paws off the wall. With that bacon still in her hand . . .

Chomp! Mmmmm! Wow, that was easy. I lick my chops.

Food Lady goes to the front closet and grabs my leash. "Hattie," she says, her face full of encouragement.

Hattie looks defeated. She trudges over to Food Lady, who rubs her shoulders.

Hooray! Hooray! We're finally going to the Dog Park.

The real one. With big water dishes to splash in. Benches to climb on. And dogs! Lots of romping dogs! I dash to Hattie's side, leaping and twirling.

She clips on the leash, and we head to the front door. We walk right past the jump rope coiled on the floor. Its scent of familiar short humans and gritty pavement has grown so faint, it's almost unrecognizable.

It's a mystery, but there's no time to investigate. There's playing to be played!

I pull Hattie down the steps and into the hot, blazing sun. After stopping to pee on a patch of grass—me, not her—we head down the walkway and onto the actual street. Where cars and trucks and buses go. I try to let Hattie know that this is a bad idea by pulling her onto the sidewalk.

But—whoa, the sidewalk is gone! Where will I find yummy crumbs to eat or sticky wrappers to lick?

Apparently, it doesn't matter, because Hattie is determined to walk in the street. Good thing there are no cars or trucks or buses coming.

In fact, it's strangely quiet. No human voices yelling or sirens screaming. And not even one car door slamming. The only noises I hear are buzzing bees and fluty, chirpy birds up in the leafy trees. It's all so wrong. Where did everything go?

And those aren't the only problems. Hattie's heading up the street . . . without Fetch Man. Or Food Lady. They're supposed to come on walks. Where are they? Why is Hattie leaving without them?

As I scout around, I see even more signs of trouble. Where are the lampposts and parking meters? Or trash cans? What will I sniff? How will I know which dogs have passed by?

The more I protest, the more Hattie yanks the leash. Maybe I'm worrying for nothing . . .

Because up ahead, beyond the trees . . . there it is! The Dog Park! I'd know that fence anywhere! My tail starts wagging. My legs move faster.

But Hattie's pace does not quicken. Doesn't she realize how important it is to get to the Dog Park? "Hurry," I bark. "The other dogs are probably already playing without us."

I sniff like crazy, trying to pick up whiffs of who might be there. My ears try to catch sounds of jingling, panting, frolicking dogs. But all I smell are chipmunks. And all I hear are more bees and birds.

Which is weird, because we're almost there. I can hardly wait! I practically drag Hattie along the fence.

I'm searching for the gate when my ears droop. My tail stops wagging. It's a park all right. A plant-y, shrubby sort of park. With a path that leads up to a porch and a house. Just like ours. No bench to climb on. No dogs to romp with.

Hattie does not smell concerned. Apparently, she knows the way.

We pass more houses, and I sense a pattern. Clusters of trees, grass, a driveway. More clusters of trees, more grass, another driveway. Where's the traffic light where we wait and sniff? Where's the fire hydrant covered with pigeon poop? We must have a lot farther to go.

We come to another plant-y, shrubby park when I do a double take. There's an animal about my size. A Perfectly Still Dog? He's got containers on either side of his back. With flowers sprouting out of them. I know every dog has his job, but let's just say I'm glad my job is not holding a bunch of flowers.

The Perfectly Still Dog is standing perfectly still, his ears spiked, his head focused forward. As if he does not even notice us. How rude!

Hattie must see him, too, but she refuses to stop. Probably for the best. We're searching for dogs to play with, and this guy doesn't seem like any fun at all.

We pause at a dense cluster of shrubs, and I take the opportunity to pee. We go past a couple more houses and driveways. Then, off in the distance, I hear a roaring, clanking sound. It grows louder and louder and louder.

Something is approaching. Hattie pulls me to the side of the road just as it appears.

I know this thing! It's the Big Brown Truck that prowls the streets and leaves packages in the lobby downstairs. But somehow it got bigger and browner. And it's truckier than I remember.

What's it doing here? Did it follow us all the way from our other neighborhood? In any case, there's no time for questions—I have a short human to protect.

I lunge at the monster, baring my teeth. "Go away, you beast! Or pay the consequences!"

Hattie gasps and yanks me out of the street. "FEN-way! Sit! Sit! *Sit!*" she yells, obviously upset by this menace.

I'm ready to attack the truck if it comes to that. I jump and growl, showing him just how serious I am. And my work pays off!

The Big Brown Truck rattles on by with a bang and a roar and a boom. Fumes linger as it cruises away— stinky, sinister fumes. "And don't come back!" I bark.

But instead of thanking me, Hattie looks annoyed. "Oh, Fenway," she says with a frustrated sigh. She must be eager to get to the Dog Park.

Hey, I'm eager, too. It's not like I asked for the interruption.

As we continue on, all I smell are birds, squirrels, and

the occasional chipmunk. I spot nothing more interesting than a stone wall, a telephone pole, or a planter of roses. My tail sinks with a terrible thought—this is not the way to the Dog Park.

Where are we going?

I redouble my efforts. I sniff every tree, every shrub, every driveway. Wait a minute! We're on the same street as before. We are passing the same trees and grassy parks we've already gone by. We pass by the Perfectly Still Dog, who's in the exact same spot as last time.

Before I know it, we end up back at our own home. Hello! We didn't go to the Dog Park. Or the place where short humans with backpacks go. Or anywhere! And we didn't come back with bread or milk. Or doughnuts. What did we do? Just wander around?

But instead of smelling frustrated or ashamed or sad that we didn't get to play, Hattie skips up the front walkway, perfectly satisfied. What is that about?

We're almost to the porch when, off in the distance, I hear the rattling, the roaring, the booming . . . louder and louder. It's the Big Brown Truck again! It pulls right up to the walk, obviously following us. How dare it return!

I spring up and bare my teeth, pulling on the leash. "I warned you not to come back!" I bark.

An Evil Human hops down from the truck, carrying a package. He heads right toward us, as if he can't even hear me.

I leap wildly. "Prepare for certain doom!"

"FEN-way! Sit! Sit! Sit!" Hattie yells, tugging on the leash. Does she have no faith in me?

As I lunge, ready to strike, the Evil Human tosses the package at Hattie. Then, he pivots and hurries back to the Big Brown Truck.

What can I say? Clearly, he was freaked out by the ferocious barking. After a horribly sinister *ROAR!* the Big Brown Truck rattles away.

"And don't even think about coming back!" I bark, swaggering up the steps after a job well done.

Hattie whisks me through the door, full of glee. She's obviously thrilled I scared away that nasty beast.

She unclips the leash, and we burst into the Lounging Place. Fetch Man stops loading books onto a shelf. Squealing, Hattie rips open the package. She pulls out something soft. A cap!

She tucks it onto her head and pulls her bushy hair through a hole in the back like a fluffy tail. She smells awfully excited about it. So does Fetch Man.

And that's not all. Hattie reaches back into the package and produces a fat glove that smells like new leather. She slides her hand into it, then starts punching it. Fetch Man grins, like he's been waiting his whole life for this very moment.

It's so disturbing. My Hattie doesn't wear a cap or a fat leathery glove. What's going on?

As I sink into the carpet, Hattie runs back and opens the front door. She calls to Fetch Man one single word: "Angel!"

CHAPTER 9

Later I'm out in our Dog Park, scratching my ear, when I spy a despicable squirrel. And then another, even bigger than the first!

The two odious rodents are chasing each other through the grass. Where they know they don't belong!

I spring to my feet. Their fluffy tails are waving and taunting. I race after them, watching them disappear into a nearby shrub. Do they actually think they can hide from me? Well, they're about to learn a Very Big Lesson.

"No squirrels allowed!" I bark, thrusting my snout into the shrubby foliage. "Do you hear me?"

But obviously, they don't. They're tumbling and battling, spitting and screeching at each other. *"Chipper, chatter, squawk!"*

"I've got you now!" I bark, plunging in deeper.

The shrub crackles and rustles. The squirrels scamper out the back and scoot across the Dog Park. Do they think they can escape? "Ha! You can't outsmart me!" I bark. I back out of the shrub, shaking leaves off my coat.

The two nasty vermin chase each other through the grass. I'm hot on their tails. They're making for the giant tree. They fly up the trunk, clacking and squawking.

I leap against the bark, panting and straining as they scurry up into the leafy branches. No doubt headed for the squirrel house to continue their fight. "Good riddance!" I bark.

Whew. That was tiring work. I curl up along one of the tree's big roots in the cool, refreshing shade. I'm about to doze off when I hear a wonderful creaking sound. I lift my head. The side gate is opening!

Whoopee! Finally, dogs are coming to play! I jump up and bolt over.

But what I see are not dogs. It's way more exciting—Hattie! And Angel! They're wearing matching caps. With long tails of hair swinging in the back. And they each have a fat glove on one hand.

Hooray! Hooray! I dash through the grass, my tail wagging out of control. "I'm so happy to see you!" I bark, jumping and pawing their legs. "I knew you'd come back!"

Hattie and Angel exchange quick glances.

"Get off, Fenway," Hattie snaps, her voice wavery and hesitant. She must be wondering if Angel will threaten our fun.

I fling myself at her knees. "Don't worry, Hattie," I bark. "We can all play together. It'll be awesome."

She sneaks another knowing look at Angel, who raises an eyebrow. What could that be about?

"Fenway, sit. Stay!" Hattie says, pointing at the fence.

What does she want to show me? I zip over there and root around in the dirt. Could there be a stick she wants me to snag?

Whatever it is, I don't have time to find out. Angel is loping through the grass. Hattie's charging in the opposite direction, punching her glove. This can only mean one thing—playtime!

Yippee! I sprint over to Hattie. Angel flips a white ball high up into the air. It falls back down into her glove with a *thump*. She looks over at us. "Ready?"

"I'm so ready! I'm so ready!" I bark. I leap. I twist. I have never been more ready.

Hattie holds out her glove. The ball goes soaring through the air. It bounces on the ground behind her and rolls into the bushes.

Wowee! Fetch is one of my favorite games! I take off after it.

"FEN-way!" Hattie shouts. And the chase is on!

I squeeze under the bush with Hattie's arm right behind me. Ha! This is too easy. I'm about to snatch it, but Hattie's hand gets there first. "Hey, I'm supposed to fetch the ball!" I bark, hurrying after her as she jogs back with the prize.

Hattie winds up and throws the ball. I'm after it like a shot. Nothing can stop me from snagging it this time, even though Angel is standing right where the ball is headed. Talk about an unfair advantage.

Angel jumps up, waving her glove. The ball sails over her head and lands with a *plunk!* in a cluster of flowers near the back fence. She tears after it. I'm close behind.

"FEN-way, stop!" Hattie yells.

Panting wildly, I arrive at the flowers just as Angel plucks the ball off the ground. Foiled again! She charges past me, clutching it in her fat glove.

I sprint after her, lunging for her arm. "No fair! No fair!" I bark.

Without breaking stride, Angel hurls the ball toward

the porch. Hattie is already there, bouncing on her toes. Another huge head start!

I bolt through the grass, my sides heaving. I've got to beat Hattie to that ball.

She swipes her glove at it, but the ball whizzes right on by. It plops near the porch and rolls under the bottom step. Hattie's shoulders deflate. With a loud sigh, she jogs after it.

Ha! I'm there first. "You won't win this time," I bark. It's the Most Fun Ever!

"FEN-way, no!" she cries as my teeth sink into the ball. She lunges for me.

But I wiggle out of her grasp. I tear around the Dog Park.

"Fen-way!" Hattie calls again, racing after me. "Drop that ball!"

I streak past the bushes and round the corner. I spot Angel rushing at me from the opposite direction. "Fen-way," she yells, waving her hands.

Clenching the hard leather ball in my jaws, I whiz around her. Hattie's hustling toward me from the other side, her arms outstretched. "Fenway!" she shouts.

I dart one way, then the other. Whoopee! Playing chase with Hattie is my favorite game, but playing with two short humans is even more fun.

Every time one of them gets too close, I swerve the other way. I rocket past Hattie. I race away from Angel. But they keep trying to catch me. They love this game as much as I do!

I'm exhausted, but there's no way I'll give up. I circle the entire Dog Park a couple more times, then realize the short humans are slowing down. Hattie is breathing hard. She glances at Angel, who is frowning.

I slacken my pace, my whole body shaking with fatigue. I drop down in the cool grass and let the slobbery ball fall out of my mouth.

Hattie folds her arms, her face gloomy. Angel is chattering, but my own panting is all I can hear.

Soon I recover enough to catch exciting sounds—
Clink! Tink! Clink!—from over the fence. I hop up and saunter over. I peer through the slats. Goldie is scratching. Patches is sniffing the ground.

"'Sup, ladies?" I say.

They look up. "Fenway?" Patches says.

"I'm not sure if you noticed," I say. "But that was me playing with those two short humans, mine and yours. They can't get enough of me."

"Playing?" Goldie's eyes are skeptical. "Is that what you call it?"

"Yep," I say. "I got My Hattie back, just like I said I would."

Patches looks curious. "How did you do that?"

"It was nothing, really." I scratch a couple of times under my collar. "All I did was save Hattie from the Big Brown Truck. Twice!"

"And you think that turned everything around?" Goldie says with a huff.

"Of course." I hold my snout high. "What can I say? She appreciates me."

Right then, the side gate bangs shut, and we all turn. Hattie is hanging her head. Angel is gone.

"So, Fenway," Patches says gently. "I don't want to burst your bubble, but . . ."

"What? Angel must've gotten tired," I say. "Hattie's still here, and we're going to play chase again. Maybe you ladies would like to watch."

Patches makes a pained face. "Um, Fenway?" she says, jutting her nose up in the direction of the giant tree.

When I turn, I see Hattie climbing up the trunk. My head droops.

"I hate to say I told you so," mutters Goldie.

I drop down into the grass and lick my paw, like that's the part of me that hurts. I hear Patches's lovely voice say, "So sad, so sad."

CHAPTER 10

Even though My Hattie bailed on our awesome game of chase, I'm still making progress on getting her back. I know I am. But that's hard to think about now. Because I'm sitting all by myself in the hallway, looking inside the Eating Place. And drooling.

Seated around the table are Fetch Man, Food Lady, and Hattie. And that's not all—Angel came back. And they're eating lots of juicy, steamy hot dogs. I love hot dogs!

I'm supposed to be under the table curled around Hattie's feet, waiting for tasty bits to fall. But I'm not. Hattie must be as down about it as I am. She's not even eating her food.

Angel's focusing her attention on Fetch Man. She chatters a lot, tossing and catching an invisible ball.

Hattie nods a few times and smiles weakly. She stares into her plate. And pushes a few beans around.

Fetch Man's eyes are wide. He chatters back at Angel excitedly. He's practically on the edge of his seat.

Food Lady gets up and offers Angel another plump, juicy hot dog. *Mmmmm!* Its yummy aroma is intoxicating.

I slurp my chops.

Angel sneaks a peek at me, then turns and asks Hattie a question.

Hattie winces like she's embarrassed. She mumbles a reply, gesturing at the Wicked Floor. Obviously explaining its evils.

Angel looks confused. Is it that hard for a short human to understand?

When the humans are finished eating, Hattie and Angel clatter their dishes in the sink. Food Lady pulls out the crinkly bag of dog food.

I spring to my feet and dance around the carpet. Oh boy! Delicious food is rattling into my dish. My mouth is salivating. Yippee! It's finally supper time!

I can hardly wait to plow into that bowl of crunchy deliciousness. "Bring it on, Hattie!" I bark, my tail out of control.

But instead of carrying it over to me, Hattie exchanges

serious looks with Angel. She sets the dish right on the Wicked Floor. "Fenway, come!" she calls, as if nothing is wrong.

My heart sinks. My tail sags. This is not how it's supposed to be. My Hattie brings me food out here in the hallway. I thought My Hattie was back.

"Fenway, come!" she calls again, crouching down and slapping her knee. Angel pats Hattie's shoulder, like she's the one who needs support.

My tummy's aching. I must convince Hattie to bring me that food. "Please, Hattie," I whine. "You can't let me starve." I flop onto my back and kick my legs. I moan and moan and moan. I turn my head for a peek.

Hattie can't take her eyes off me. She looks like her heart is breaking. Angel pats Hattie's shoulder some more.

Hattie is clearly torn. She murmurs something to Angel, then grabs the dish and hurries into the hall.

Wowee! I knew she'd do it! I plunge right in like someone's about to stop me. *Mmmmm!* It's the Best Meal Ever. Sadly, it disappears all too soon.

"I knew I'd get My Hattie back," I bark. I lick and lick her cheek. She smiles.

Angel plops next to us on the carpet, shaking her head. Her face looks disapproving.

I climb onto her knee and lick her anyway. She tastes like ketchup.

When everything's cleaned up, we all head to the front door and Hattie clips my leash. She goes for the jump rope, but when Angel frowns, she drops it. Hattie sighs and grabs the fat leathery glove instead.

Whatever she has planned, it's bound to be fun. When we get outside, Hattie leans down to hug me and somehow my leash gets tied around a slim tree. "Um, hey, Hattie . . ." I bark as she walks away. "Aren't you forgetting somebody?"

Hattie stops near a patch of dirt, where Food Lady is kneeling and digging and sprinkling water. Angel is near the driveway, fingering that white ball. Which can only mean one thing—another awesome game of fetch! Or chase! I struggle to get loose.

Fetch Man hovers next to Hattie, watching her intently. He has a hopeful look in his eye.

"Hey, everybody!" I bark. "In case you haven't noticed, I'm stuck here and I can't play."

They act like they can't hear me. Angel winds up and hurls the ball toward Hattie and Fetch Man. Hattie stretches out to get it, but it bounces behind her and dribbles toward Food Lady and the dirt.

"I'm on it, you guys!" I bark, leaping out as far as I can. It's a whisker beyond my reach.

Hattie jogs right past me, looking annoyed. Or discouraged. She scoops up the ball and heads back.

"Unfair! Unfair!" I bark. I jump and twist, even though it's no use.

Fetch Man rests his hand on Hattie's back. He talks into her ear, then stands aside, moving his arm like he's tossing a ball.

Hattie nods. She strokes her cap a couple of times. She pulls her arm back and flings the ball at Angel.

Fetch Man starts clapping, but then stops as the ball sails over Angel's head. It lands on the driveway and begins rolling toward the street.

Hattie's shoulders slump. Fetch Man pats her back, his face encouraging.

Angel is about to head after the ball when strange sounds make us all stop in our tracks.

Tinky-tinky-tink-a-too.

Is it music, like fluty birds? It's moving toward us. It must be exciting because Hattie and Angel drop their fat gloves and squeal with glee. Do they know what this is?

Fetch Man does not appear the least bit curious. Food Lady does not even look up. She keeps on playing in the dirt like her sense of hearing is gone.

The *tinky-tinky-tink-a-too* is getting louder. And closer. Hattie skips up to Fetch Man, who digs into his pocket. Smiling, he hands Hattie and Angel a couple of small flimsy papers.

Clutching them tightly, the short humans scamper to the edge of the grass. Their heads turn in the direction of the noisy music. Waiting.

Until . . . a truck turns the corner!

My hackles shoot up. Is the Big Brown Truck coming for us again?

No! It's smaller. And whiter. And it's playing the tinky-tinky music.

Hattie and Angel hop up and down, their arms waving.

"Hattie, stand back!" I bark, leaping and flailing. "This thing must be dangerous!"

But she is not listening to my very obvious warnings. The truck stops right next to the short humans, who are not moving out of the way. He's going to get them!

"Go away! We don't want you here!" I bark at the truck.

Like the Big Brown Truck, this one has a human inside. He leans out the window. Hattie, full of energy, talks to him. So does Angel.

"Run away!" I bark to the short humans. "Go inside, climb a tree, anything!"

Can they not hear me? Fetch Man or Food Lady,

either? Fetch Man is over at the dirt chatting with Food Lady like everything's fine.

Good thing I'm here to save the day. Except for the Very Big Problem of the leash. I pull and pull, but there's no way I can reach Truck Man. All I can do is bark. "You'd better scram, or else!"

Hattie gives him a flimsy paper. Angel does, too. And just like that, Truck Man disappears. Was he scared off by my dire warnings? Or the short humans' chattering?

Unfortunately, neither. Truck Man returns and shoves something at the girls. Angel bounces impatiently. She reaches her hand toward the window. Is she trying to push Truck Man back inside?

"I told you to leave!" I bark. Even though it's useless, I lunge with all my might and—*snap!*—the leash breaks off!

I rocket across the lawn. I'm heading right toward that truck at full speed.

Food Lady and Fetch Man spring up. They race over, too, like they suddenly realize the danger the short humans are in. "Fenway! Fenway!" they're calling, as if I'm not already on the job.

I arrive at the scene just as Angel has apparently figured out that she's no match for the musical truck. She turns to me, her eyes wide. Hattie starts shouting and waving her arms.

"FEN-way! Stop!" Food Lady and Fetch Man both scream.

"Go away! Leave these short humans alone!" I bark, baring my teeth. I'm leaping higher than I've ever leaped before. I must reach that window!

I leap extra, extra high, but I still can't reach it. As I fall back down, I collide with Angel, who lets out a shriek. Next thing I know, white creamy globs are all over her clothes.

Truck Man is yelling. Food Lady and Fetch Man are practically breathless. But somehow this does not prevent them from speaking very loudly.

Angel pulls at her delicious-smelling shirt like it's on fire. I taste a few drips as they fly off. *Mmmmm!* Sweet and frosty. I go in for a better lick.

Angel jumps back. Her face is angry. "Bad dog! Bad dog!" she yells.

Hattie squats down and grabs what's left of my leash. She shakes her finger at me. "FEN-way!" she says with a very mad "you're in trouble" voice.

What'd I do? No time to find out. My nose is detecting an irresistible blob of ice cream on the pavement. Talk about a distraction. *Mmmmm!* Vanilla!

Chapter 11

The bright morning sun is shining through the window. I go to nuzzle Hattie, but she's not there. And worse—this is not even her bed. Where am I?

A quick glance around confirms the shocking reality—I'm in an empty room. Trapped by The Gate!

Suddenly, I remember a horrifying dream. Hattie bossing me in here last night, brandishing The Gate. Wait a minute! Did that really happen?

No! Hattie doesn't boss. Hattie doesn't brandish The Gate. I begin tearing around the room. Pictures are flying into my head. Images too awful to be true.

Could I have actually spent the whole dark night alone in this strange room? Was I really curled up on this hard, wooden floor instead of in Hattie's comfy bed that smells like mint and vanilla? With no Hattie brushing my fur and singing "best buddies" as I'm falling asleep? Did I even sleep?

I'm panting and shuddering. I can't stop racing in circles. It's worse than a nightmare. Finally, I get ahold of myself. There must be something I can do.

I rush over to The Gate. "Hello!" I bark. "I'm in a boring place, and I can't get out!"

I bark and bark, but nobody is coming. I pause and listen. Are those the sounds of my humans shuffling around downstairs?

I must keep at it. I bark and bark some more. When I stop to listen again, my tail starts going nuts. Footsteps are coming up the stairs. I knew my plan would work!

I leap up, trying to peer over The Gate. Those footsteps are getting closer, and then . . . Hattie appears. "Hooray! Hooray!" I bark, offering my head for the rub. But where is it?

I fall back down. Hattie has her arms folded, her face a terrible mixture of irritation and disappointment. Why is she glaring at me like that?

She definitely could use her adorable dog's help to get rid of that frown. I jump and jump, trying desperately to lick her hand. "I have a great idea, Hattie," I bark, cocking my head in that cute way she likes. "Let's go to the Dog Park and have some fun!"

She leans away. "Stop it," she says in a sharp voice.

I collapse in a heap of confusion. What is happening to My Hattie? My heart's so heavy, I might sink right through the floor.

Hattie talks in a serious and scolding voice. She does not sound anything like My Hattie. She sounds a little bit like Food Lady does when I climb on the couch.

Hattie speaks and speaks, using lots of Human words I don't know. They are pelting me like rocks. I can't even look at her. All I can do is cover my eyes and sulk.

When Hattie leaves, I'm alone for a Long, Long Time. But then, there's good news—Hattie is back! She removes The Gate and scoops me into her arms. Yippee! She's My Hattie again. I lick her chin and her neck and her ear.

But my hopes quickly crash when we get outside. She sets me down and strides right over to that giant tree. She must be hibernating in the squirrel house, because after I've sniffed every inch of the Dog Park and peed on every shrub, she's still up there.

Eventually, there's nothing to do but sprawl out in the grass and listen to the fluty, chirpy birds and buzzing bees. And wait for Hattie. It's the Loneliest Dog Park Ever.

I'm half snoozing when my ears perk in annoyance.

"Chipper, chatter, squawk!"

My fur prickles. It's one of those nasty squirrels. This one is even bigger than the two from last time!

He's scampering across the tippy-top of the fence, along the far side of the Dog Park. Doesn't he realize there's a ferocious dog guarding the place?

He's obviously not very smart. Because every time he reaches the end of the fence, he pivots and darts back the other way. But then again, who ever said squirrels were smart?

As he scurries along, his hissing grates in my ears. His twitching is almost too revolting to watch.

But I can't run away from my duty. I must defend my territory. I'm a professional.

I spring up and trot closer. But not too close. "Get out of here, you disgusting rodent!" I bark. "A Dog Park is no place for squirrels!"

He is not acting the least bit intimidated. He stops mid-scamper and bares his squirrel-ish fangs right at me. *"Chipper, chatter, squawk!"* he screeches. The sound is pure evil.

I'm a few paces away but still within striking distance. "I said, 'Go away!'" I bark, with more urgency this time.

"*Chipper, chatter, squawk!*" he screeches again, as if he even has a chance against me. Digging his vicious claws into the top of the fence, he thrusts his hideous face in my direction. He's going to fling himself right at me!

I back up a little, every hair on my neck trembling. "You're not welcome here, you cowardly beast," I bark. "Now beat it before I destroy you once and for all!"

But my serious threats do not drive him away. Next thing I know, that little monster flies off the fence, right into the Dog Park! As soon as his feet hit the grass, he scampers toward the giant tree.

Ha! If that's how he wants to play, he picked the wrong opponent. "I've got you now, you nasty creature!" I bark, taking off after him.

His fat, fluffy tail swishes tauntingly as he runs. I can already taste that disgusting fur in my jaws. I'm about to snap when he flees up the trunk in an ominous racket of clickety-clacky-clacks. Uh-oh! Hattie's up there!

I paw the bark of the giant tree, snarling and growling furiously. "Leave Hattie alone, you menace!" I bark. "Or you'll have to answer to me!"

Fortunately, the rustling and swaying branches tell me he has enough sense to avoid the squirrel house. I drop down in the shade and curl up for a well-deserved rest.

Then my ears detect familiar sounds through the fence. The jingling of dogs. If only I could get excited.

"Is that you, Fenway?" Patches's lovely voice calls.

I slump a bit lower.

"He looks like he lost his best bone," I hear Goldie mutter.

"Poor guy," Patches says. "It reminds me of the first time our sweet Angel left the leashes on their hooks, forgetting all about them. You parked yourself at the door and sulked and stewed and didn't move. Not even at supper time."

"Me?" Goldie huffs. "I believe you were the one who whimpered and carried on like a puppy when she went out without us that day. She practically shut the door on your nose, like you weren't even there."

Patches sniffs. "She ran out without giving us so much as a pat."

"Well, a dog can't keep living in the past," Goldie says. "What's done is done."

Patches sighs. "Still, I can't help but remember the good times."

"What's the point?" Goldie says, then calls over to me. "Hey, Fenway. Do yourself a favor and move on without that short human. You're only making yourself miserable."

"Have a little sympathy," Patches says. "Can't you see the pain he's in?"

It's all too much to bear. "Leave me alone," I cry.

"See?" Patches says.

"Hey, I'm only trying to help," Goldie says. "Is it my fault if the little guy won't listen to my advice?"

"There's advice and then there's wise advice," Patches says.

"And I suppose yours is wise?" Goldie grumbles.

"Fenway," Patches says kindly, "we know from experience how hard it is to move on. But believe me, life without your short human isn't as bad as you think."

"That's your wise advice?" Goldie says.

Patches ignores her. "Listen, Fenway, at first, we couldn't accept it. But as time went on, we got used to entertaining ourselves."

"That's right," Goldie says. "Instead of swimming in the pond, now we lie in puddles."

"You mean we splash in the wading pool," Patches corrects.

"Speak for yourself," Goldie says with a growl. "I lie in puddles."

"In any case," Patches goes on, "we've found ways to adjust. And you will, too."

I want to ignore them, but a sense of fury rises up

through my fur and consumes my entire body. In a flash, I'm charging over to the fence. "Maybe that's working for you," I say. "But I could never live without My Hattie. I am going to get her back."

"Now, Fenway, I know you're determined, but . . ." Patches says, her eyes sad and wincing. "Have you actually thought about what a gargantuan task that would be?"

"Hey, maybe he's some kind of super dog," Goldie says with a sneer.

"I know you both think I can't do it," I say. "But I can! I will! Maybe I just need more time. Or better ideas. Or something. But I'll do it. Just you wait."

"Would you listen to him?" Goldie murmurs.

I jump up and scratch the fence. "And who knows?" I say, feeling a surge of power. "When I get My Hattie back, maybe I'll get your Angel back, too."

Patches gasps, but then her face falls. "If only we could have our precious Angel back," she says sadly. "It's all I wish for."

"Too bad it's impossible," Goldie says, then looks away suddenly. Like she doesn't want us to see her drooping ears.

I know I'll do it. I have to. All I need is a plan.

@Hapter 12

Just then, the sliding door bangs, and I jump. Fetch Man is on the porch, his fat leathery glove on his hand and a familiar cap on his head. He tosses a white ball into the air and catches it. Okay, he's no Hattie, but playing ball with Fetch Man is my second favorite thing to do. "Excuse me, ladies. I have a game to play," I call over my shoulder, trotting to the porch.

"Go knock yourself out," Goldie says.

"Goldie . . ." Patches scolds.

Fetch Man grabs another fat leathery glove off the porch. He bounds down the stairs, holding it out in the direction of the giant tree. "Hattie," he calls excitedly.

I'm leaping at his side for a better sniff. And view.

The glove on Fetch Man's hand smells old and worn.

It looks bigger than the other one, which is new and stiff. Fetch Man beams proudly. Like he's found a bone that was lost for a Long, Long Time. "Hattie!" he calls again.

Her face appears in the squirrel-house window, but she does not look happy. Hattie grimaces and shakes her head.

Fetch Man reaches out the glove, like he's not sure Hattie saw it the first time. "Come on," he begs.

Hattie shakes her head more forcefully.

Fetch Man sighs loudly. Then he chatters in a voice that sounds like a combination of coaxing and pleading. Like he's trying to get her onto the cold, scary scale in the vet's office.

Next thing I know, Hattie's face vanishes from the window. Her sneakers appear beneath the leafy leaves. She's coming down!

"Hooray! Hooray!" I bark, romping over. "We're all going to play fetch. It's the Best Day Ever!"

Fetch Man's right behind me. The instant Hattie's feet touch the ground, he hands her the glove.

"Oh no," I hear Goldie say.

"I can't bear to watch," replies Patches.

"It's okay, ladies," I say, prancing near the fence. "I've got this. Just you wait."

Patches looks like she wants to say something but changes her mind. Goldie drops down and scratches.

I charge back over to Hattie. "I'm so ready! I'm so ready!" I bark, leaping on her legs.

"FEN-way," she snaps. She turns to Fetch Man, whose voice has changed from coaxing and pleading to serious and guiding.

Really, Fetch Man? You think Hattie doesn't know how to play fetch? It's one of her favorite games!

"Let's go! Let's go!" I bark, circling their feet. "What are we waiting for?"

"FEN-way, stop," Hattie snaps again.

Hey, can you blame a dog for being impatient?

Hattie trudges back to the porch and grabs her cap. She tucks it on, pulling her bushy tail through the back. "Ready," she says. But she sure doesn't sound like it. Or look like it. For one thing, she's standing way too close to Fetch Man, giving me a huge head start.

I trot into the middle of the grass, waiting for Fetch Man to wind up and send the ball flying toward the back fence.

But instead, Fetch Man leans in. He flips the ball gently toward Hattie's chest.

She slaps at it with her fat glove, but it bounces off and lands in the grass. Hattie hangs her head.

"I'm on it!" I bark, speeding after the ball as it rolls behind Hattie's feet.

She can't resist the chase. She snatches it practically right out of my jaws—in a way that is not very playful.

Fetch Man pats Hattie's arm. He straightens the leathery glove on her hand. He punches his own glove a few times. He takes a couple of steps back and nods.

Hattie's face is sheepish. She takes a loud breath. Her hand goes back for the toss.

I'm so ready! I'm so ready! I take a lead toward Fetch Man, bouncing and panting. I can hardly wait!

Hattie hurls the ball toward us. I race after it. So does Fetch Man.

Only he's running backward. He leaps way up high, stretching his arm overhead. He grunts and grunts and—*thump!* The ball smacks into his glove.

"No fair! No fair!" I bark, springing up like I could possibly reach the ball in Fetch Man's hand.

Fetch Man clutches the ball like a prize. He grins at Hattie. "Nice!" he shouts happily.

Hattie does not share his enthusiasm. She shakes her head and scowls. *"Nice?"* she asks, her voice full of disbelief.

Fetch Man's shoulders soften. He walks back toward her. "Prack-tiss," he pleads over and over. Finally, she nods.

He backs up a couple more steps. He makes an excited face. "Ready?" he says.

"I'm so ready! I'm so ready!" I bark, jumping wildly at his feet.

Fetch Man bends his knees. He softly tosses the ball right to Hattie. Even though she's standing there all stiff and nervous and not ready at all. And I'm the one who obviously wants to chase it.

Hattie swipes at the ball. It taps the side of her glove and drops gently into the grass. She groans.

"Mine! Mine!" I bark, preparing to pounce.

But once again, Hattie grabs the ball before I have the chance. I leap at her legs as she straightens. She squeezes the ball in her glove. She's not even looking at me.

I jump higher. "When is the fun going to start?" I whine.

"Fenway," she says, her hand shooing me down.

"Come on! Come on!" I bark, dancing around her sneakers. "I want to play, too."

Fetch Man glances at Hattie, raising an eyebrow.

She lets out a sigh, hands him the white ball, and races toward the sliding door.

"Whoopee!" I bark, behind her all the way. "Chase is my favorite game."

But the door slams shut just as I reach it. I turn and

watch Fetch Man flip the ball over his head and catch it a few times, perfectly content. Isn't he upset that Hattie ran off?

A moment later, the door opens and Hattie reappears with my leash. Are we going to walk to the real Dog Park?

"Yippee!" I bark, leaping up and licking her knee.

As the leash clicks, Hattie hops down the steps toward the side fence. I'm galloping along beside her. Wheeeee! The breeze ripples through my fur as we run through the grass. It's the Best Feeling Ever!

But when we get to the fence, the wonderful feeling abruptly ends. I go to follow Hattie back to Fetch Man, but—*ouch!*—my collar tugs me back. Somehow my leash got wrapped around a slat in the fence. "Hattie, help!" I bark. "I got stuck!"

As if she can't even hear me, Hattie tosses the ball back and forth with Fetch Man. Gently and seriously, like it's not even a game. Or any fun.

Hattie is working and struggling, not playing. And she looks so . . . discouraged.

If only I could get loose. I could show her how much more fun it is when the ball whizzes far over our heads. And we have to chase after it a Long, Long Way.

I crumple into a heap of helplessness. And defeat.

"I hate to say I told him so," Goldie mutters.

"He has to learn for himself," Patches says.

My ears perk up. "What do I have to learn?"

Patches looks like she doesn't know what to say. Or maybe how to say it.

Goldie nods toward Hattie. "You can keep trying all you want, but she's not going to be the same short human you had before. She's changing."

I want to tell them they're wrong. That I'm going to find a way to get her back. All I need is a good idea . . .

Then I hear "Woot! Woot!"

I whip my neck around. Hattie is jumping around in a fit of celebration. Her fist is gripping the white ball, pumping the air like a sign of victory. Even from here, I smell a feeling I haven't smelled in a while. Confidence?

Fetch Man grins and claps his hands.

Patches lets out a little whimper. "It's so painful to watch. So very like our own sweet Angel with that same white ball, the same glove . . ."

Goldie shakes her head in disgust. "That's how it went wrong. It all started with that ball and glove . . ."

Whoa, the ball and glove are the problem?

I spring to my feet. I thrust my nose into a gap in the fence. "I told you I'm going to get My Hattie back," I say to the ladies. "And I know exactly how to do it."

Chapter 13

When we head inside, I can hardly believe my nose! The unmistakably wondrous aroma of spaghetti and meatballs is wafting out of the Eating Place. Saliva pools in my mouth. Yippee! It's supper time!

But as Hattie hangs my leash on the hook, I swallow my excitement. I can't let myself get distracted. I have a plan to get My Hattie back, and nothing will stop me.

Fetch Man hangs up his cap and the two fat leathery gloves. The big one over his cap, the smaller one over the leash.

I watch Hattie and her swinging tail of hair rush into the Eating Place. My nose is overwhelmed by the savory fragrance in the air. I love spaghetti and meatballs!

But I have a mission to focus on. I slink back to the door. Those gloves are up awfully high.

I leap my highest. I stretch myself as far as my body will go. No matter how hard I try, there's no way I can reach. And *sniff, sniff* . . . aaaaah! That spaghetti smells sooooo good. And I'm sooooo hungry . . .

I want to go beg Hattie to bring me some, but I can't get distracted. Getting My Hattie back is too important!

I jump and jump and jump. I can almost reach the end of the leash. I try again, my jaws snapping.

At last! I chomp on the clasp and give it a tug. Did Hattie's glove shift just a tiny bit?

I look way up. It's slightly off-balance. I have to keep at it!

I'm about to tug some more when I hear food clattering into my supper dish. My tummy grumbles.

"Fenn-waay . . ." Hattie's sweet voice sings.

I want to stick to my task, but my belly's in charge. I bolt over to the Eating Place doorway.

My dish of sumptuous food is sitting in the middle of the Wicked Floor. Hattie's gazing at me with eyes full of determination. "Fenway," she calls. "Come!"

I thrust my snout through the doorway. My tummy is rumbling. I look at Hattie with my saddest, droopiest eyes. I give her my best whine. "Don't you feel bad for me, Hattie? I can't get to my food and I'm staaaaarving."

But instead of bringing it to me like she's supposed

to, she doesn't even flinch. She keeps on staring. "Fenway, come," she calls again, clapping her hands.

Uh-oh. Something's wrong. Hattie's not looking at me with sympathy and concern like she always does. And she sounds almost . . . commanding. Convincing?

I glance at my food. Sitting there in the dish. Smelling so delicious. Waiting for a ravenous dog to come devour it.

But that Wicked Floor stands between us. Talk about torture!

I drop down and whimper for a Long, Long Time. For all the good it does. Hattie keeps on calling me, again and again. Like I'm miraculously going to defeat the Wicked Floor, charge on in, and gobble down the food.

Why won't she just bring it to me?

It's horribly unthinkable. My Hattie's changing like Goldie and Patches said she would. I have to get her back. I have to work harder.

But right now I'm famished. And exhausted. I curl up for a rest.

And then, everything changes. Hattie comes over and grabs the leash.

I hop up. "Hooray! Hooray!" I bark, pawing her legs. "We're going somewhere!"

We all pile into the car. I'm so excited, I almost forget

how hungry I am. Until I get a whiff of Hattie's backpack. Wowee! It's loaded with treats! Good thing I'm starving!

I lick her cheek, then stick my nose out the window as we zoom down the street. My eyes squint in the warm breeze.

When the car stops, my tail wags out of control. Because my nose is smelling amazing familiar smells.

We're at that Treat Place again! Where I'm going to get treats! And see my new friends. "Come on! Come on, Hattie!" I bark, clawing the door. "Let's get going!"

We barrel out of the car, and I lead Hattie across the parking lot. When we get to the door, I see Lance, the Yellow Lab, from last time.

"Yo, dude," he says as we politely exchange bum sniffs.

"Hey, Lance. What's up?"

"No idea," he says. And the look on his face proves it.

Lance's human pulls the door open, and we head inside. It's that same big room that smells wonderful. And the same dogs from before are there with their humans. Sadie, the very round Beagle, is lying on her side like it's nap time, while Rocky, the Basset Hound, is trying to drag his human back out the door.

Food Lady and Fetch Man get busy chatting with the other humans. I steer Hattie around to greet my new friends. "Wake up, Sadie," I say after sniffing under her tail. "The treats are coming, remember?"

She raises her head with considerable effort. "Trust me, honey," she says. "I remember. But those tasty morsels better come easier this time. I've had it with exertion."

When we get to Rocky, he's actually shaking. "Relax," I tell him. "There are going to be awesome treats."

"Fenway, you are way too happy about this," he says with a shudder.

"What's not to be happy about?" I say, hopping up and sniffing Hattie's backpack a few more times. "Is something wrong with your ears, Rocky? I said we're getting treats!"

He gazes up at his human like no treat could possibly cheer him up. I can't help but wonder why he wants to go home so badly. Does he live atop a pile of steaks?

When the One Human strides over, the rest of the humans immediately give her their full attention. She obviously has some kind of power over them.

Hattie takes in a deep breath. Like she's getting ready for something.

I'm getting ready, too. I'm leaping and leaping, pawing her legs as she unzips the backpack. Hooray! Hooray! Those treats are coming!

My mouth waters. My tummy roars. I didn't eat supper, but now I'm getting treats! A whole backpack full of them.

"Whoopee!" I bark, dancing around Hattie's sneakers. "I can hardly wait!"

Hattie balls her fist and holds it over my head. "Sit, Fenway!" she says.

I spring up wildly, sniffing like crazy. Sure enough, a tasty-smelling treat is in her hand. I know it is! "Give it to me, Hattie!" I bark. "What are you waiting for?"

Hattie looks rattled. "Sit!" she says. "Fenway, sit!"

"Yippee!" I bark, jumping on her legs. I can almost reach her fist. "I can already taste that delectable treat!"

But Hattie's fist remains closed. With that treat still inside. "Sit, Fenway," she says again, her eyes getting watery. "Sit! Sit! Sit!"

I nuzzle her hand in a desperate attempt to open it. "I'm so ready! I'm so ready!" I bark.

Next thing I know, the One Human is hovering beside us. She smells like lots of dogs and treats, but she also smells serious. And her voice is bossy. Hattie is completely focused on her. The One Human finishes speaking, and Hattie nods.

Then, with no warning at all, Hattie turns. She stares into my eyes, takes a deep breath, and holds her fist right over my nose. "Sit," she demands. Her voice is full of conviction.

Whoa, she wants me to do something. But what? Her posture reminds me of that time when I sat and the

One Human gave me a treat. I plop down on my bum, my gaze never leaving her fist. When it opens, I'm not going to miss the yummy snack.

Hattie bounces up and down. "Yes!" she shouts. And just like that, the treat falls into my mouth.

Chomp! Wowee, is it ever tasty! I'm crunching and munching that meaty morsel in a state of pure happiness that ends all too quickly.

Hattie smiles at the One Human, who pats her shoulder. "More, please!" I bark.

Hattie holds another treat above my nose. "Stay!" she orders, then takes a step back.

Hey, I'm not going anywhere.

"Yes!" she shouts again, and a wonderful treat sails into my mouth.

Chomp! Oh boy! It's just as yummy as the last one. It's another blissful moment of crunching and munching that I wish would never end.

Fetch Man and Food Lady are grinning. They pat Hattie on the back. Hattie smells proud. Like she won a competition. Or a battle.

They must be awfully happy that I finally got some food. And they're not the only ones. My belly is on fire. I can hardly wait for more.

Hattie is totally distracted by Fetch Man and Food Lady, which can only mean one thing—opportunity.

I sniff my way over to Hattie's backpack. My nose tells me it's stuffed full with treats. And it's right behind her on the floor!

I thrust my entire head inside. Wowee, this thing sure is loaded. I knew it!

Chomp! Chomp! Chomp! I'm wolfing the treats one after another after another. I can't stop. And why would I want to? There are enough treats here to last forever. I'm in a bagful of Dog Heaven!

"FEN-way!" Hattie yells.

Ouch! My collar is tugging at my neck, pulling me right out of the backpack. "Hey, what'd you do that for?" I bark, wiggling to get free.

Hattie's face is frowning. Her shoulders are heaving. She's struggling to breathe. Big fat tears start sliding down her cheek. Something tells me that treat time is over.

Chapter 14

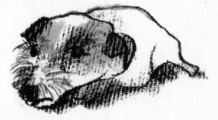

Bright morning light assaults my face.
My eyes pop open.

I dig my front paws into the floor and stretch waaaaay back. I walk my hind legs in and thrust my chest waaaaay out. I look around.

Hey, I'm not in Hattie's bed! I'm in that same boring room from yesterday. Did I sleep in here again?

I trot over to the door, and there's more bad news. It's blocked by The Gate. What'd I do to deserve this? Where is Hattie?

I try to remember . . . riding home in the car, Hattie gazing out the window . . . bossing me up here, clicking The Gate . . .

I give a little yelp. The memories are almost too

agonizing. Another night all alone, curled up on the hard, wooden floor. What happened to my bedtime fur brushing? Hattie's sweet voice singing "best buddies, best buddies"? Or the soft, comfy blankets that smell like mint and vanilla? Are they gone for good?

One thing's for sure—this is not how it's supposed to be. I have to do something. I have to get My Hattie back.

I position myself at The Gate. "Hattie! Hattie!" I bark as loud as I can. "Please help me! I'm trapped, and I have to get out!" I add an extra howl or two to make my point.

But when I stop, all I hear is quiet. I start to think that maybe she's actually gone away and is never coming back. But then I catch the sounds of my leash jingling and footsteps charging up the stairs.

"I knew it! I knew it!" I bark, spinning in circles. I'm so relieved, I almost forget to rush over to greet her. "I missed you so much!"

Hattie bends down and lifts me over The Gate.

I lick her cheek, but she turns away. She smells annoyed.

She sets me on the floor and goes to clip the leash.

Hooray! Hooray! We're going for a walk. I leap up, pawing her legs. "I can hardly wait!"

Hattie frowns. "Fenway, sit!" she says.

Wowee! A treat is coming! I twirl around with hungry anticipation.

"Sit!" she snaps, trying to steady me with her hand. Which does not have a treat inside.

I spring out of her grasp. I sniff her pocket. Where is the treat?

Hattie lets out a loud sigh. She grabs my collar and clips the leash with a frustrated huff. Next thing I know, we're hustling down the stairs.

We head out the sliding door, into the back Dog Park, and straight over to the bushes. Hattie stands still, waiting.

Come to think of it, there is some business I need to attend to.

I'm barely finished when I detect a nasty whiff of squirrel. Nose to the ground, I search for the trail when my collar tugs and—

Hey! Hattie's dragging me through the grass and up the porch steps. "What's the hurry?" I bark. "We just got here."

But she must not hear me. She pulls me inside and back up the stairs into the boring, empty room. Behind The Gate.

Without a pat or a rub, she disappears.

I sink onto the floor. Why is Hattie doing this? Why is she changing? Why can't she stay My Wonderful Hattie forever?

I curl back into a ball to continue the Most Boring Day Ever. I must drift back to sleep for a while. Because when I open my eyes, sounds are floating in from the window. I dash over to investigate.

Thump! "Yes!" Hattie's joyful voice yells.

I must find out what's going on. I climb onto a box near the back wall. I leap up and up until my front paws cling to the window ledge. Balancing on the tippy-tips of my hind paws, I peer down through the screen into the Dog Park. I spot the grass, the fence, the giant tree in the back. They all look so much smaller for some reason.

Hattie and Fetch Man are standing at opposite ends of the Dog Park, caps on their heads. Each has a fat glove on one hand. Fetch Man goes into a windup like he's going to throw a ball for a game of fetch. Only he has no ball.

Hattie nods. She clutches her glove to her chest. She reaches into the glove and pulls out a white ball. Then she winds up exactly like Fetch Man did and tosses it toward him.

He leaps up, thrusting his fat glove way out to the side. *Thwaaap!* He snags it and claps the glove with his other hand.

"Yes!" Hattie cries. She dances around, waving her arms.

I start to pant uncontrollably. My humans are playing in the Dog Park while their loyal dog is trapped up here inside a boring room. They are acting happy, like they're having fun. Like they don't even realize that somebody important is missing. This is so wrong. I must do something!

But then, my ears pick up other sounds. From over the fence.

Clink! Jingle! Jingle!

Wowee! Talk about distracting. Right next to our Dog Park is another one just the same. With grass and bushes and a fence all around it. It doesn't have a giant tree in the back, but it does have two dogs in it—a Golden Retriever and a white dog with black patches. Hey, it's the ladies!

They look perfectly content, too. Goldie is sniffing in the bushes. Patches is rolling on the ground. Everybody is having fun, and I'm stuck here all alone.

Or am I?

"All-rite!" comes from nearby. Hey, somebody else is up here, too.

I turn way to the side, above the ladies' Dog Park. Peeping out an open window the same level as mine is the head of a short human. With a cap and a long wavy tail. Angel?

She's watching Hattie and Fetch Man. Grinning and pumping her fist.

Why is Angel up in the window when the ladies are playing down in the Dog Park? That's not the way it's supposed to be. It reminds me of Patches's sad voice. *"It's so painful to watch. So very like our own sweet Angel with that same white ball, the same glove . . ."*

Hattie hugs her own fat glove like it's a used-to-be bear. Or an adorable dog.

Another human's voice sounds from directly below my window. Food Lady!

Fetch Man turns and flips the ball to Hattie. She reaches forward and scoops it into her glove. She smiles again.

Fetch Man jogs toward the house and vanishes from view. I hear the door slide open and bang shut.

Hattie twirls around, happy as can be. She throws the ball up into the air and watches it fall—*thump!*—into the fat glove. Again and again.

My ears flop with sadness. My short human is playing by herself. It's not right. Doesn't she need me?

"Please, oh please, Hattie," I whine. "Let's play ball together like we did before."

Hattie looks up. She scowls, one hand on her hip, then shakes her head. She goes back to tossing the ball. Like that's the only thing she wants to do. Or cares about.

"Oh please, pleeeeease, Hattie," I cry. "I'll let you win. I promise!" I scrape my claws on the window ledge. I jump higher, my claws poking the screen . . .

Hattie snaps her head up in alarm. "FEN-way!" she shouts. She races toward the house and quickly disappears. I hear the door thud.

"Hooray! Hooray!" I fly off the box and tear around the empty room. "I knew she'd come!"

Soon Hattie arrives at The Gate. "FEN-way," she scolds.

How am I in trouble? There isn't even anything to do here.

When she scoops me up, I go crazy licking her cheek. "I'm so glad you're back," I bark between slurps. She tastes like salty sweat. And something else, too. Confidence again?

I'm so happy to be back in Hattie's arms, I nestle against her neck all the way down the stairs and through the house. The more she speaks in that stern un-Hattie voice, the more I snuggle.

By the time we head out the sliding door, she's stroking my back. I knew she couldn't resist her super best friend. She sets me on the porch, and I dance around.

"Yippee!" I bark. "We're finally going to play!"

But maybe Hattie's had enough playing. The door closes, and she's gone.

My heart crashes. What just happened?

I can't go on like this. I have to get My Hattie back. For good.

I plop down for a quick scratch when suddenly I realize the opportunity I've been waiting for is sitting right next to me on the porch.

CHapter 15

I stare at the fat glove for a second or
two. I can't believe I've finally come face-to-face with it.
Prepare for certain doom, you no-good Glove! You are
the cause of all the trouble.

Snarling, I bare my teeth. I take a running leap. I
pounce!

Clenching it tightly in my jaws, I whip my head
from side to side. The Glove is stiffer and heavier than I
thought. And way more leathery.

I let it drop to the porch floor. Time for the real work.

I creep slowly around the perimeter of the Glove,

my gaze firmly upon its smooth surface. Its weakness is here somewhere. And I will find it.

Aha! I spot a bit of string, like a leathery shoelace. It's the perfect place to begin. And as I examine the Glove more closely, I see more of them.

Lots more. Probably millions!

Could this be the Easiest Job Ever? I chomp down on the nearest bit of string. I tug and tug with all my might. I will not relent!

But the string is not budging. I have to stop and rest, panting like a weakling. Until I spot a more vulnerable-looking piece right next to it.

I'll get you, you other piece of string! My teeth have been preparing a lifetime for this very situation. *Chomp!*

I pull and pull. My jaws are tired, but they will not give up. I steady the Glove with my front paws and dig my weight into my hind legs. I tug my head back and back and back.

For a Long, Long Time, I keep at it. Now and then, I hear the ladies' voices next door muttering to each other. "What's going on over there?"

But there's no time for socializing. Nothing will distract me from my goal. After more and more biting and pulling, I hear an encouraging ripping noise. Progress?

With each tug, the string rips a little more. I pull and pull and pull. At last, a bit of the end breaks off. I spit it onto the porch, panting and drooling.

I glare at the Glove, inspecting the damage. Other than a few teeth marks, it looks exactly the same as before. One thing is clear—there's a lot more work to do!

Luckily, there are millions of strings left. I'm biting and chomping and chewing till my jaws are aching. I spit out more and more pieces. Others are fraying and tearing. They are no match for a determined dog like me!

I'm exhausted, but I have important work to do. I have to finish the job. I must!

Eventually, my tongue is slobbering. My lungs are panting. My sides are heaving. I stand back to admire what's left of the Glove.

Most of the strings are ripped or gone. The fat leathery part is full of holes and tears. There's no doubt about it—this Glove has been sufficiently attacked.

I sink down onto the porch. All I want is a well-earned nap in the sun.

But for some reason, the ladies choose that exact moment for conversation. "Fenway?" Patches calls, sounding concerned. "Is everything all right?"

Somehow, I find the energy to trot over to the fence.

"Everything's way better than all right," I say, thrusting out my chest. "Actually, everything is perfect."

Goldie snorts. "Really?"

"Hattie won't be playing with that Glove anymore. And she probably won't be climbing the giant tree, either. She's going to be My Hattie again, just like always. Thanks to me."

"You sound pretty sure," Goldie says. "How can a dog change a short human?"

"Maybe you've never tried," I say. "Or maybe you didn't have the right plan."

"Oh, and you do?"

"I don't want to brag or anything. But let's just say I'm not afraid of hard work."

Goldie gruffs. "Are you calling us lazy?"

"Hey, I'm not judging you."

"It's just that we'd hate to see you get your hopes dashed," Patches says.

"Not that we'd know anything about that," Goldie says.

"The fact that you lost your Angel and couldn't get her back has nothing to do with me and My Hattie," I say. "It's like comparing balls and Frisbees."

"Fenway," Patches says, hesitating like she's not sure she should continue. "We've been trying to be delicate. We've been trying to be understanding and supportive.

But it's time for you to own up to the truth. Nothing can bring a short human back."

"Maybe you don't want to admit that you failed with your Angel," I say. "And you're jealous that I'm going to get My Hattie back."

"Now wait just a minute there, little guy," Goldie says with a snarl. "We are not jealous."

"We're only trying to help," Patches adds.

"Why don't you save your helpfulness for somebody who needs it?" I shout. "My Hattie's coming back to me. Everything will be the way it's supposed to be. Just wait and see."

"Humph," Goldie says.

The sliding door thuds, and we all turn. Hattie! And Angel!

"Looks like we're about to get that chance," Patches says.

"Watch and learn," I say to the ladies. I rush up the steps.

The short humans scamper onto the porch, wearing caps with tails of hair swinging from the back. Angel has a fat leathery glove on one hand.

"Hooray! Hooray! It's playtime," I bark, jumping and leaping at Hattie's legs. "I'm so glad you're back. I missed you so much."

But instead of reaching down and petting me, Hattie

stands up tall. She gives Angel a quick glance, then looks at me. "Sit," she says in a commanding voice as I paw her shins. She points to the floor.

She's trying to tell me something. But what? Are there treats on the floor? How could I possibly have missed them? I circle around and around, busily sniffing the area around Hattie's feet. I must find those treats!

"Um-oh-kay . . ." I hear Angel say.

I keep on sniffing, but I do not smell any treats. What's going on? All I smell are those leathery bits from the Glove.

Apparently, Hattie notices them, too. "What?" she cries, hurrying to the corner of the porch and grabbing the Glove. She turns it over, examining the destruction.

Angel joins her. She leans in, her hands on her hips.

Hattie's whole body sags. Clearly, the Glove has let her down.

It worked! My tail goes nuts. Hattie won't want to play with that Glove anymore. Now we can play chase. "Come on, Hattie!" I bark, bounding down the porch steps. "Try to catch me!" I start running through the grass.

Sure enough, she's hot on my tail. Angel, too. I knew it was the Best Idea Ever, but I have to admit, it's working even better than I thought.

"FEN-way!" Hattie yells.

Around and around we go, zigging and zagging all through the Dog Park. My ears blow straight back. My fur ripples in the breeze. My tongue lolls to one side. I sure hope the ladies are watching. I hate to say I told them so, but . . .

"FEN-way!" Hattie screams even louder, pretending to be mad and growly. She loves playing chase as much as I do. It's our favorite game!

I'm racing around the giant tree when I see Angel coming at me from the other way. Ha! Does she think I'm an amateur? I instantly twist and reverse directions.

But when I come out the other side, there's Hattie. And Angel's still behind me. They've got me cornered!

It's important to win, but there are worse things than being nabbed by My Hattie. And besides that, I'm officially trapped.

As she scoops me into her arms, I go to lick her cheek. She makes a sour face. And she smells mad. Super mad.

Chapter 16

Whoa, I'm the one who lost the game.

Why is Hattie upset?

She holds me up at arm's length. She gazes at me intently, her eyebrows narrowed. "FEN-way!" she yells, louder and madder than ever. She keeps on yelling and yelling. She does not even sound like Hattie. She sounds like somebody I don't know.

And she looks like somebody I don't know, too. Her shoulders are tense and her hands are trembling. Her face is puffed and furious. Her eyes are pooling with wetness.

"Bad, bad dog!" she cries, her breath becoming uneven. Her voice is a horrible mixture of fury and grief.

Tears start spilling down her cheeks. "Bad, bad dog!" she wails between sobs.

My ears are sagging, my eyes wincing. It hurts too much to look at her face. Even my fur is drooping with sadness. I try to shrink. I try to recoil. But she's holding me tight, and there's nowhere to hide.

"Bad, bad dog!" she cries over and over, like she's the one who's in pain.

Why is this happening? Why is Hattie angry at me? We were playing chase, her favorite game. We were having fun. I even let her win.

Hattie turns my face back toward hers so I can't look away. She keeps saying those terrible words, "Bad, bad dog," right into my eyes. Like somehow I'm going to understand.

"I can't bear to watch," Goldie mutters.

"Or listen," says Patches.

And I was beginning to think things couldn't get worse. The ladies were right. Hattie's changed. And now on top of this horrible agony, I have to suffer humiliation, too.

All I want to do is run away. I try to wriggle out of Hattie's grip, but she only clutches me tighter. It's by definition the Most Awful Day Ever. I hang my head and whimper. When will it end?

And just like that, Hattie sets me down. She flies up the porch steps, charges into the house, and slams the door.

Angel gives a little cry of surprise, then bolts after her.

I curl up in the grass, covering my eyes. If I could get any smaller, I'd actually disappear.

"My heart is aching for him," Goldie murmurs.

"I wish there were something we could do," Patches says.

A bee buzzes overhead, happy as can be, like all that matters is the next flower. "Please go away," I yelp.

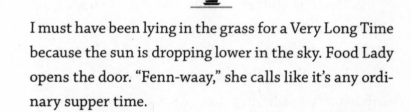

I must have been lying in the grass for a Very Long Time because the sun is dropping lower in the sky. Food Lady opens the door. "Fenn-waay," she calls like it's any ordinary supper time.

Hey, maybe it is an ordinary supper time? Maybe whatever happened is over now. I trot inside and poke my head into the Eating Place.

My supper dish is filled with food all right. But it's in the same spot as usual—on the Wicked Floor. And that's not the only bad news. Fetch Man's at the table, but where's Hattie? Is she gone?

I must find her! I blast around the corner and fly up the stairs. When I get to Hattie's room, I'm wildly out of breath. And wildly relieved.

Good news—she's in there! I want to dance around in celebration, but something horribly suspicious is going on.

Hattie is opening drawers and packing things into a bag. I go to inspect them, but she grabs my collar. "Stop it," she scolds, pulling me away. She grabs a rolled-up blanket from the closet. I chomp one end for tug-of-war, but Hattie sneers. "Stop it!" she yells again.

I slink back. Hattie's upset. And she's packing things. It can only mean one thing—she's leaving!

She must be stopped. Food Lady and Fetch Man are either unaware or not up to the task. As usual, the job falls to me. If only I knew what to do.

Hattie grabs her cap and goes to toss it into the bag with her other stuff. But then she stops. She scowls and tosses it on the dresser instead.

She looks around the room as if searching for other things to pack. I follow her gaze to the bed. Aha! The used-to-be bear! That's how to stop her!

I bound up and snatch it. I hop off and run around the room. Ha! Hattie can't leave now.

Hattie hurls the bulging bag over her shoulder. She hugs the rolled-up blanket.

I prance in front of her, waggling the used-to-be bear. I prepare to take off the moment she goes in for the chase.

But she barely notices. She heads for the door and races down the hall.

Whoa, how did that not work? I drop the used-to-be bear and race out of the room. It's all I can do to keep up with her.

She dashes into the Eating Place, where Fetch Man and Food Lady greet her with concerned faces and lots of chatter. Fetch Man's voice is soothing. Food Lady's sounds more like pleading.

Hattie clutches the blanket roll to her chest. Her body is tense and trembling like her hackles are raised. She shouts angry words for a long time, tears sliding down her face. Finally, she stomps her foot. She glares at them, waiting for them to respond.

But they are quiet. Fetch Man hangs his head, then looks up at Food Lady with sad eyes. She gazes back at him, her hand on her forehead. Fetch Man opens his mouth to say something, but doesn't. Food Lady's eyes get watery.

What's wrong with them? Can't they see that Hattie's running away? They're not even saying anything. Why aren't they trying to stop her?

Food Lady shrugs her shoulders like she has no choice

but to give up. Fetch Man sighs loudly and puts his arm around her. "Let-ter-go," he says.

I have no idea what he just said, but they're not doing a thing. They're just letting her go. Hattie can't leave. I must find a way to stop her!

Fetch Man speaks to Hattie in a warning voice. He goes to a cabinet and takes out a small light. Food Lady opens another cabinet and pulls out a bottle that I recognize right away. It makes an awful hissing sound and sprays a smelly, choky mist. I back off, even though there's no way she can reach me.

Hattie marches to the sliding door. Fetch Man and Food Lady follow with the small light and choky spray. Are they actually helping her leave?

I have to do something. I can't let my short human run away!

I'm running in circles, desperate for an idea, when I spot Hattie's rolled-up blanket. And her bulging bag.

Right in the middle of the Wicked Floor.

How long before she realizes she's forgotten them and heads back? I could steal that blanket. The bag, too! I could hide them where she'd never look!

She wouldn't be able to leave.

It's the Greatest Idea Ever!

But I have to hurry. She could be back any second.

I'm about to race into the Eating Place when the flaw in my plan hits me like a door in my face.

Her things are on the Wicked Floor.

I've faced this situation before. And I did not win.

But the stakes have never been higher. There must be a way!

I dart back and forth in the hallway. How can I force the Wicked Floor to surrender Hattie's things?

I'm exhausting myself from racing and pacing. But I'm a professional. It's my life's work to protect my humans from danger. I can't let a Wicked Floor keep me from doing my job.

I swipe a paw across its evil surface. It's smooth and slick as ever, but a dog's gotta do what a dog's gotta do.

I plant both paws onto the floor's gleaming wickedness. Instantly, my brown paw slides away. The white one buckles awkwardly under my chest. I crumple—*splat!*—across the doorway. "Ouch!" I yelp. "Eee-yowww! Eee-yowww!"

My hind claws dig into the carpeting. I ease myself back out into the safety of the hall. I try to lick the soreness out of my paw. Too bad I can't lick away what's really hurting. Hattie is running away without me. I stop mid-lick to growl at the Wicked Floor. "I'll get you," I bark. "Somehow."

Hattie bursts back into the Eating Place as determined as ever. Although judging by the nauseating smell, she lost a battle with the choky spray. She rushes over and collects her bag and rolled-up blanket. She turns and heads out. I hear the back door slide open. She does not say good-bye. She does not even look back.

I race around the corner to the door and peer through the screen.

Hattie climbs up the giant tree. And then . . . she is gone.

Chapter 17

Without Hattie, nothing matters. Nothing will ever matter again. I slink down, gazing helplessly out the door. When Food Lady and Fetch Man come back inside, they practically trip over my lifeless body. My muscles wouldn't move if I bribed them.

Which is apparently what my humans are trying to do. "Fenn-waay," Food Lady coos, sweet as cream. She strides into the Eating Place, gesturing at my supper dish. Like I could've possibly forgotten it's there.

Fetch Man waves a piece of kibble under my nose. I cannot even bear to sniff it. He presses his hand against my side. As I let out a deep sigh, he smells relieved.

They head into the Lounging Place. I hear the familiar *click!* and sounds from the Flashing Screen.

Later, Fetch Man comes back and opens the sliding door. "Fenway," he says, more authoritatively this time. When I don't bother getting up, he carries me outside and waits until I water one of the bushes.

Through the darkness, we both steal glances at the giant tree. But there's no sign of her. Just a nasty squirrel skittering along the side fence.

Fetch Man shrugs and brings me back inside. When he closes the door, I press my nose into the screen. As if I'll suddenly see her climbing down the tree and running back to me. I can't suppress a whimper.

"Fenway," Fetch Man says with a sigh. He pulls me away from the door and deposits me in the hallway. Out comes The Gate. The lights go dark. And I am alone.

I'm lying in the hallway for a Very Long Time. Eventually, my eyelids get heavy. I close them for just a second. And then . . .

I'm out in the Dog Park. With the biggest hot dog I've ever seen. It's the size of our car. And it's glistening with hotdog-y goodness. Just waiting for me to race over and take a bite.

Wowee! How did I get so lucky? I can't wait to sink my teeth into it.

I go to chomp one end, but suddenly, the whole hot dog disappears. Hey, where did it go? It's completely vanished.

I'm searching for it everywhere when over at the fence I see a flicker of pure horror.

Squirrels! Lined up on the fence. More squirrels than I've ever seen. They're enormous. Gigantic. It's the Scariest Sight Ever!

One very fat, very nasty squirrel leads the pack. His belly is huge and bulging. His teeth are long and fanglike, dripping with squirrely saliva. I can't look at him without shuddering. He is the definition of evil.

"Chipper, chatter, squawk!" the Evil Squirrel screeches. He scurries down into the Dog Park, and the rest of the pack follows. They're invading!

A Dog Park is for dogs. I open my mouth to frighten them away, but no sound comes out. What happened to my bark? I'm speechless!

Pretty soon, the Dog Park is completely packed with gigantic squirrels. But they're not teasing or taunting or daring me to chase them. They don't even notice me. What's up with that?

Clearly, they have a plan. The Evil Squirrel scampers over to the giant tree. The others race after him. They shoot up the trunk and into the leafy leaves. They're headed for the squirrel house.

A shiver runs from my snout to my tail. Hattie is up

there. The Evil Squirrel bares his fangs. The others raise their claws. They are about to enter the house. Hattie's in danger!

A squirrel-y face pops out of the little window, her eyes wide with fear. I know those eyes. It's Hattie!

She's turned into a squirrel!

I wince in horror, every hair on my coat shuddering with disgust. My sweet, lovely Hattie, my favorite short human of all, has become one of my mortal enemies!

I gaze out across the Dog Park. Hattie's eyes are full of terror. She's trapped. She's afraid. She needs me.

Squirrel or no squirrel, she's still Hattie. I'll never stop loving her.

Especially now that she's in trouble. Those gigantic squirrels have her surrounded. There's only one thing to do—I have to save her!

There must be a way. If only I could bark! At least I can run. Or can I? My legs won't move. Come on, paws. Let's go!

They will not budge. They must be attached to the ground. It's worse than being trapped. I'm officially useless.

I can't just stand here. Time is running out. The pack of gigantic squirrels is perched on the branch. Which is bending and bending and bending.

I hear a loud rushing, whooshing sound. And then . . .

. . . CRRRRR-ACK!

Or is it click?

Whatever it is, it's followed by a pounding, splattering sound, like sheets of rain. And BOOM-KABOOM!

I shiver. It's all so terrifying. I can hardly stand to listen. But then I hear different sounds . . . tip, tap, tap.

My eyes pop open, but . . . suddenly everything is dark. I can't bark, I can't move, and now I can't see!

And hey—the grass feels exactly like cushy carpeting.

It *is* cushy carpeting! I'm no longer out in the Dog Park. I'm back in the house. In the hallway outside the Eating Place.

Is this real? Or is it a dream?

In any case, there's no time for questions. The *tip, tap, tapping* is getting closer. It's inside the sliding door.

And it's moving. Into the Eating Place.

Good thing there's nothing wrong with my hearing.

Rain pelts against the window. A light flashes outside. For an instant, I can almost make out a large lumpy, bumpy creature.

Inside the Eating Place.

It smells like damp tree bark. And wet leaves.

This can only mean one thing—it's that Evil Squirrel!

He's come inside to stop me from saving Hattie. Like he actually could! Short human or squirrel, she's still my beloved Hattie. And nothing can stop me from saving her!

BOOM-KABOOM!

I leap up. Hey, I can move! "Out of my way, Squirrel!" I bark. "I have a job to do." Hey, I can bark!

But the Evil Squirrel is not intimidated. His shadowy shape keeps slinking through the Eating Place, determined to stop me.

Not if I stop him first. I'll charge right in and show him who's boss. But when my paws cross the threshold, I realize there's another Very Big Problem.

Chapter 18

The Wicked Floor!

How could things get any worse? Hattie's in trouble. An Evil Squirrel is trying to keep me from saving her. And the Wicked Floor is in my way.

I can't let it stop me. I won't!

Hey, wait a minute! What am I thinking? I can go the other way!

"I'm coming, Hattie!" I bark. In a flash, I'm halfway down the hallway. I'm almost there! But then I meet another obstacle—The Gate. It's blocking my way to the door!

I can't get through, but I can't give up. There's too much at stake. Before I can talk myself out of it, I race back toward the Eating Place. There's only one thing to do.

I muster every ounce of courage I have. I dig in my claws and crawl inside the doorway, fighting to keep my balance. "I'm warning you for the last time, Squirrel," I bark. "Go away or face the consequences!"

The Evil Squirrel turns toward me and freezes. He gives a slight "shhhh." Is he scared? Or about to make his move?

There's no time to take chances. I must strike first. I take a couple of stumbling steps. I'm scrambling. I'm slipping. I'm going down.

But no—I must save Hattie! I keep racing ahead. Nothing can get in my way. I'm hurtling toward the Evil Squirrel. My paws slip and slip, but I pull myself up. "Hold on, Hattie!" I bark.

When I get close, I bear down on my front paws. I lunge at the Evil Squirrel. "Prepare for certain doom!"

Obviously frightened, he gasps.

My cue to pounce! I paw the Evil Squirrel's lumpy, bumpy fur. Which does not feel very furry.

He holds out an arm . . . That's his defense?

I throw myself at him again, nipping, pulling, tugging. Until he is scared right out of his skin.

Literally! As the Evil Squirrel shrieks in horror, the lumpy, bumpy covering slides off his body. Which smells awfully familiar, like mint and vanilla. And a bit like that choky spray . . .

Hattie?

Is my nose deceiving me? I back off. I cock my head and glance up into the wonderful dark eyes that I'd know anywhere.

It IS Hattie!

"Fenway," she says. "Sit!"

My gaze locks to hers as if pulled by an invisible leash. I sink onto my bum, my tail thumping the cool, slick floor.

"Good boy! Good boy!" Hattie squeals. She drops to her knees, squeezing me and patting my head.

I slobber her nose and her eyes and her chin. Hooray! Hooray! My Hattie came back, and she's not a squirrel anymore. And best of all, she's loving me again.

Hattie rubs my belly, laughing and showering me with kisses. It's a deliciously happy moment that I hope will never end. She missed me so much, she can hardly do enough to show it. And wowee, the love and appreciation sure feel great.

"I missed you, too," I bark. I'm nuzzling Hattie's wet hair—where's her cap and bushy tail?—when my ears perk.

Whooshing, howling noises are coming from outside. Suddenly, I remember the gigantic squirrels.

I race over to the sliding door. I peer out, but there's only blackness and pounding rain. In the few flashes of light, all I see is an empty Dog Park. And the giant tree's leaves rippling and blowing in the wind.

Those evil squirrels are gone!

Clearly, they were petrified. "And don't even think about coming back," I bark in triumph.

When I rush back into the Eating Place, it's bathed in bright light. Food Lady's rubbing her eyes, and Fetch Man's wearing his glasses. They look like they just woke up.

"Hattie," Food Lady says in a voice that sounds glad but mostly relieved. Honestly, you'd think discovering that Hattie has returned would be cause for a full-blown celebration.

Fetch Man says, "Fenway!" He sounds surprised. Did he forget about me?

Hattie speaks very quickly. She must be explaining to Food Lady and Fetch Man what happened—that she turned into a squirrel and a pack of rival squirrels invaded her house, but a fierce and loyal dog frightened the squirrels away.

And in case they couldn't figure out who the hero is, Hattie gestures dramatically toward the middle of the floor where I'm standing. With a huge smile on her face.

Gosh, I almost feel embarrassed.

Food Lady's eyes bulge. Her hands fly up to her mouth.

Fetch Man squats down, grabbing his knees. His face is beaming. "Good boy!" he says, more surprised than ever.

"Good job!" Food Lady rushes over and gives me a tight squeeze. Fetch Man joins in.

Hey, it's all in a day's work, I want to say. No squirrel has a chance against me. But then again, I could get used to the lovefest.

And then, right when I thought things couldn't get any better, a spectacular sight comes into view—my supper dish. It's filled with food! Did I forget to eat it?

Food Lady must be reading my mind, because she lets me go at that very moment. I shoot over and start wolfing it down like it's the First Meal of My Life. And *mmmmm*, is it ever tasty.

Apparently, my humans are just as ecstatic about the food as they were about my heroics. Hattie jumps up excitedly. Fetch Man puts his arm on Food Lady's shoulder. They are all standing over me, mesmerized. Like they've never seen a dog eat before. And frankly, it's more than a little distracting.

Hattie strokes my back. She smells happy and proud. It's the Best Smell Ever.

I gaze at my empty bowl, wondering how the food disappeared so fast. And that's when I see something else that makes my tongue start panting . . .

The Wicked Floor!

My bowl is sitting right on it. And so am I.

This can only mean one thing—I have trounced my nemesis. I am the winner!

For such a Long, Long Time, the Wicked Floor ruled the Eating Place. But not anymore. Its reign is officially over.

I flop down and rest my face on its cool surface. I rub my nose on it. Take that, you Wicked Floor! You may be Terrifying and Evil and Slippery, but you're no match for me.

Chapter 19

When the morning light is blazing, I climb over the cozy blankets to nuzzle Hattie.

"FEN-way," she growls, though she smells anything but growly. I lick her face until her eyes flutter open. She's here. My Hattie's here. And we're curled up in her bed. Together. The way it's supposed to be.

After another Walk to Nowhere and returning without bread or milk or doughnuts, me and Hattie go outside to play in the Dog Park. "Fenway," she says, pulling her hand out of her pocket.

Whoa, she's got my attention. I leap and leap, poking my nose toward her fist. *Mmmmm.* It smells delicious!

She puffs out her chest and gazes into my eyes. Her expression is full of love. And power.

A persuasive combination. I'm listening.

She opens her mouth. "Sit."

Hey, I know that word. A beautiful memory pops into my mind. I sink onto my bum as Hattie's face breaks into that huge grin I know so well.

She holds out her arm and takes a step back. "Stay," she commands.

Ha! I know that word, too. I sit still and wait for it.

And the treat drops into my mouth. *Chomp!* Wowee, it's completely amazing!

Just like the hug Hattie gives me. "Good boy, Fenway!" she cries, kissing my head over and over. She smells as thrilled as I feel. Who knew it was so easy to make a short human this happy?

The rest of the day, we play ball and chase. We eat treats that Food Lady makes. And later, after we all enjoy a tasty supper in the Eating Place, Fetch Man and Food Lady head to the garage door. Hattie grabs my leash. We're going for a ride in the car! This awesome day keeps on getting better.

As soon as the car stops, my tail starts going nuts. We're at the Treat Place!

I lead Hattie inside, full of happy anticipation. Friends. Treats. Hattie. What more could a dog want?

When we pass Lance, he gives me a nod. "Dude!" he says.

Rocky is trying to drag his humans back out the door. "Cheer up," I tell him. "Treats are coming."

Sadie cocks her head in my direction. "Fenway, where do you get your energy?"

Hattie smells cautiously optimistic. Like she wants to be in charge, but she's not going to push. And her backpack is bulging with treats. I can hardly wait for the fun.

When the One Human enters, the others focus on her immediately. And the dogs are focused on their own humans. Because of the treats.

And after the One Human finishes speaking, the only sound in the room is a chorus of thumping tails. We are so ready. Cue the treats.

Hattie puffs herself up, strong and tall. She holds out a fist. She points to the floor. "Sit," she commands.

I know this! I know this! I plop onto my bum and wait for it. The treat drops into my open mouth. *Chomp! Mmmmm!* How easy was that?

Hattie's whole face grins. She smells as pumped as I feel.

"Stay," Hattie says, her voice even more confident than before. She takes a step back.

Hey, I'm not going anywhere. Her hand tosses the treat and—*chomp! Mmmmm!*—oh yeah, that's tasty. Hattie's smile is so radiant, it makes me feel warm.

We do the exact same thing over and over. Each time, Hattie's voice is stronger and more confident than ever. And my tummy is happier and happier, just like My Hattie. Food Lady and Fetch Man stand over us, watching. Their faces are beaming with pride.

And that's not the only good news. We have loads more fun when the One Human comes over and shows me and Hattie how to play lots of other games. Hattie tells me "Down," and I lie down, "Leave it," and I ignore a toy, and, best of all, "Come," and I rush into her sweet arms. She's happy, I'm happy, and the treats just keep on coming. It's an awesome slice of paradise until . . .

"Yo, man!" Lance is barking. "I said, 'Where's the treat?'"

We all turn at once. Lance is jumping on his human, who is flailing his arms and shouting. "Hey! Get down! Off!" This guy's either totally lost it, or he's about to.

I catch Lance's eye. "Chill out, dude," I tell him. "Your human needs you."

Lance stops and tilts his head. "Needs me for what?"

"To make him happy."

Lance looks totally surprised. Did he not expect me to be the source of such wisdom? Or is he stunned by the simple message?

Whatever the reason, he gets it. He gazes eagerly at his human, who is visibly relieved and says, "Sit."

His tail swishing, Lance sinks to his bum. Yes! A treat sails into his mouth. He smacks his chops.

Lance's human lets out a whooshy breath. His face is beaming with joy.

Lance bows his head for the rub. And another treat.

Rocky turns to me, impressed.

Sadie stares, admiring my cleverness. Or maybe just checking me out.

What can I say?

After many more treats and, even better, lots more pats and hugs of happiness from my humans, we get back in the car. I snuggle onto Hattie's lap. I soak up the praise all the way home.

CHapter 20

The next morning, we head out to walk.
But something's different. Instead of turning up the
street as usual, Hattie and Food Lady go in the opposite
direction. Is this the way to the Dog Park? My nose gets
busy sniffing for clues.

And right away, I find some! In the grassy park next
door, I smell Golden Retriever and another breed I can't
quite identify. Goldie? Patches? Is this where they live?

My tail starts going berserk. And with good reason.
Hattie and Food Lady turn into the front walkway. I
pull them toward the house.

The door opens and out steps Muffin Lady. And
Angel. And more good news! Goldie and Patches. On
leashes.

Wowee! My whole body wiggles with excitement. "'Sup, ladies?" I say.

Our noses and tails go wild with friendly greetings.

"I almost can't believe it," Goldie says as we bound down the porch steps. "Angel's coming on a walk with us. After all this time!"

"I'm so full of hope," Patches says in her lovely voice. "Maybe our precious Angel isn't lost to us after all."

"Never lose hope," I say proudly. "I didn't. And now I have My Hattie back."

"What could've happened?" Goldie says.

"Get this," I say. "Turns out she was changing all right. Into a squirrel!"

"Horrors!" the ladies gasp.

"Yeah, it was pretty frightening. But luckily, I saved her. In the nick of time."

"You saved her?" Goldie says.

"What did you do?" Patches says.

"It was nothing. Just doing my job."

"Tell us," Patches says.

"Let's just say I can be pretty ferocious when I put my mind to it."

Goldie looks like she wants to disagree but thinks better of it. "Wow."

"Fenway," Patches says in her loveliest, most admiring voice. "You're a hero."

Awww, shucks.

The humans get busy yapping as we head into the street. Goldie and Patches do not think this is a bad idea. And I confess I'm getting used to it.

The humans turn and go in our usual direction. I hope the ladies don't think we're headed Somewhere. I'm tempted to tell them the bad news that we're not going anywhere cool like the Dog Park, but I don't want to spoil our perfect day.

As we stroll up the street, I can't help thinking this is the way it should be. Walking together, like a family. We're in the zone, ears back, eyes straight ahead. Except for the humans, who are chatting, not looking where they are going, and dragging on the leash. In other words, not behaving at all. But somehow, it's okay.

When we pass by the grassy park with the Perfectly Still Dog, he's still there. Ears perked high, gaze fixed. Carrying the same flowers in the exact same spot, like he's never even moved.

"What do you suppose is his deal?" I ask the ladies.

"What?" they both say at the same time.

"Him." I cock my head toward the Perfectly Still Dog.

Goldie and Patches exchange glances. They must be as perplexed as I am. Patches looks like she wants to say something but doesn't.

Then Goldie says, "Fenway, you've got an interesting way of looking at things."

"Thanks." I guess.

We pass a few more grassy parks, trees, and bushes, then stop at a driveway where a Lady Human is rubbing sudsy water on a car. Food Lady and Muffin Lady chat with her while a short human skips across the grass, her black, silky hair bouncing behind her. She plops beside me and strokes my head. "Awww," she coos. "Puppy!"

Clearly, this short human appreciates a handsome dog. I lick her cheek, and she giggles. She smells like glitter and glue.

She smiles at the short humans. "Zah-ra," she says.

Hattie nudges Angel, her eyes wide. She smells like she's getting an idea.

Farther up the street, my ears pick up a familiar sound.

Tinky-tinky-tink-a-too. That musical truck! It's headed straight for us!

Hattie and Angel must recognize it, too, because their energy surges. They hold out their hands to the tall humans, who give them flimsy little papers.

Hattie and Angel bounce on their toes, eagerly awaiting the truck's arrival. Obviously, they are ready to confront the monster like a couple of ferocious dogs. I guess they've been inspired by a certain canine hero.

But can they handle this evil on their own? I hardly have time to decide. The musical beast appears, its tinkly voice blaring. "Go away, you nasty truck!" I bark, leaping and thrashing wildly. If the leash weren't holding me back, I'd . . . I'd—

"FEN-way!" Hattie shouts. She's pushing her palm toward the pavement. "Down!"

I know this! I know this! I drop to the ground and lie at her feet.

Hattie pats my head, her body radiating total happiness. "Good boy! Good boy!" she says. She sounds deliciously wonderful. Just like the treat that sails into my mouth.

The ladies look on, impressed. What can I say?

And the short humans are just as successful in getting what they want. Clearly intimidated, the Evil Human disappears from the truck window and then returns with ice cream. Which Hattie and Angel snatch right out of his hands. That's my girls!

As we watch the musical truck cruise off into the distance, I sidle up next to Hattie. Thankfully, I don't have to wait long. A nice glob drops right in front of my paw. *Sluuuuuuurp! Mmmmm!* Vanilla.

Back at home, another amazing thing happens. Me and Goldie and Patches head through the side gate and into . . . the Dog Park!

Hooray! Hooray! I romp with the ladies, tumbling and tussling and chasing for a Long, Long Time. It's the most fun at the Dog Park ever! Eventually, we flop down in the cool grass for a rest. I lay my head next to Patches. She licks my nose.

I'm considering a well-deserved snooze when sounds come from the front of the house. Short-human sounds.

The ladies spring up. We all flock to the side gate to investigate.

The short human we met on our walk is skipping up the driveway, a sparkly headband on her head. Hattie and Angel are rushing to greet her. "Zah-ra," they cry. Hattie's waving. She's holding the jump rope.

Hattie hands one end of the jump rope to Zahra. Angel goes to take the other, but then shakes her head, a huge grin spreading across her face.

Hattie's eyebrows arch, but then she starts grinning, too. She and Zahra grip the handles and stand far apart. Soon the jump rope is turning and slapping the pavement in a steady beat. Hattie begins chanting in a singsong rhythm. The others chant along with her.

The jump rope circles over, around, and under a very happy Angel again and again and again. Angel hops up and down, grinning widely as the jump rope turns and slaps, slaps, slaps the driveway.

"Aha," Patches says. "So it's a game!"

I cock my head. "What do you mean?"

"Angel's been hopping over a rope like that for days and days," Goldie explains.

"We couldn't figure out why," Patches says.

Goldie's fur prickles. "Maybe you couldn't. I always knew it was a game."

"As I recall, you were just as puzzled as I was," Patches says.

"Humph," says Goldie.

A happy squeal directs our focus back to the gate. We watch the jumping, chanting short humans for a while, then Goldie snatches a stick and takes off. Me and Patches chase her around the Dog Park.

When it's dark outside, I finally have Hattie all to myself. I'm cuddled in her soft and cozy bed. She kisses my brown paw, then my white paw. She showers my neck with kisses. I slobber her cheek, and she giggles.

Hattie brushes my fur and sings, "Best buddies, best buddies . . ." It's the Happiest Moment Ever. Me and My Hattie are together forever, and nothing can come between us.

Sighing with contentment, I close my eyes. And then . . .

I'm sprawled out in the soft and cozy grass.

"Chipper, chatter, squawk!" *An Evil Squirrel climbs over the fence, his sharp, drooly fangs glistening in the moonlight.*

I sprint after him.

"Chipper, chatter, squawk!"

"It's called a Dog Park for a reason!" I bark.

He scurries toward the back fence. Where Hattie is crouched down in the grass. Her arms wide open . . .

"Watch out, Hattie!" I bark.

But it's too late! That Evil Squirrel jumps right into her arms!

"Awww," she coos, caressing his bristly fur.

He chippers softly and snuggles against her neck.

No! No! Somebody please tell me Hattie's not actually cuddling that nasty creature!

He looks back and glares at me. He opens his mouth . . .

CRRRRR-ACK! BOOM-KABOOM!

Whoa! That's one loud squirrel!

My eyelids pop open. Whew! I'm in Hattie's soft and cozy bed, shuddering. A bright light flashes outside. Rain pounds on the window. This cannot be good.

Hattie's clutching the used-to-be bear. She reaches for me. "Best buddies," she whispers.

Shaking with courage, I crawl onto her chest. I nuzzle against the used-to-be bear. Hattie strokes my back. Making Hattie happy is a big job. But luckily, I'm a professional.

Acknowledgments

In the midst of my own family's chaotic move from the suburbs to the city, I found a way to cope by journaling as a dog named Fenway. Eventually, those notes turned into a character, and his story became a book—after a lot of hard work and with the help of many, many people.

All of them deserve treats.

A pile of meaty bones to my Super Agent, Marietta Zacker, the greatest champion any characters (or author) could ever have. Not only did she believe in Fenway from the very beginning, but she encouraged me to dig out more of Hattie's story, and in the process, we dug out more of Fenway's story, too.

A platter of juicy hot dogs to my Editor Extraordinaire, Susan Kochan, who opened her arms and welcomed Fenway and Hattie into the Best Home Ever. With enthusiasm and patience, not to mention brilliance, she fed and cared for them, gave them plenty of fun and exercise, and even taught them a few new tricks as they prepared to go out into the world.

A basketful of chew sticks to the fabulous editorial team at Putnam and all the talented people at Penguin Books for Young Readers for their countless hours of hard work and creativity in making this story into a book. Every one of them has earned an extra walk, plus a carefree game of Frisbee at the Dog Park!

A room full of squeaky toys to my amazing writer friends, who embraced Fenway at first sniff, eagerly tossed the ball without tiring, remained stubbornly loyal through slobbery messes and unmentionable mishaps, and even held his paw at the vet's office once or twice. A loud round of squeaks go to Hillary Hall Debaun, Sheri L. Gilbert, Joe Lawlor, Cynthia Levinson, Cheryl Lawton Malone, Judy Mintz, Pat Sherman, Pamela de Oliveira Smith, Donna Woelki, my classmates from Grub Street Boston, and my very wise and generous teacher Ben H. Winters.

And best of all, a long, joyous romp on the beach for my family: Ralph, Philip, and James. A writer and her dog could never know more incredible support, longer-lasting patience, or greater love. I hope I've given you lots to be proud of. And laugh about. XXOO.

Victoria J. Coe grew up in the seaside community of Duxbury, Massachusetts, and went on to live in New York and San Francisco, as well as large and small towns on both US coasts. During her family's most recent move, she noticed her dog's confusion and started to wonder what was going through his mind. As they walked in Boston's Fenway neighborhood, his reactions to the sights, sounds, and smells of the city took hold of her imagination. Although she has written for many publications and nonprofit causes, authoring her first novel for children is the realization of a life-long dream. Victoria now lives with her family on the outskirts of Boston, where she and her dog are always on the lookout for delivery trucks. And squirrels.

www.victoriajcoe.com
instagram.com/victoriajcoe
Twitter: @victoriajcoe